Tina gri ~~~~~ **r seat and wille** ~~~~~ **You can't f** ~~~~~ **he said, her** ~~~~~

Nico leaned back and spread his hands to encompass their surroundings. "Can I not? We are on an island. The only way on or off is by helicopter or boat—and I control both of those things."

Her stomach plummeted through the stone floor of the terrazzo even as a chill shuddered through her. "You're being purposely contrary. My brother will come looking for me. You can't prevent that."

Nico took a leisurely sip of wine, studying her through lowered lids. She endured the scrutiny, though he reminded her once more of a great cat toying with its prey. She sat very still, waiting for him to spring, knowing she was caught even before he did so.

All she could do was wait and see what manner the attack took.

"No," he said finally, "I can't stop Renzo from looking for you. But even he cannot separate a man and his wife."

Lynn Raye Harris read her first Mills & Boon® romance when her grandmother carted home a box from a yard sale. She didn't know she wanted to be a writer then, but she definitely knew she wanted to marry a sheikh or a prince and live the glamorous life she read about in the pages. Instead, she married a military man and moved around the world. These days she makes her home in North Alabama, with her handsome husband and two crazy cats. Writing for Harlequin Mills & Boon is a dream come true. You can visit her at www.lynnrayeharris.com

Recent titles by this same author:

UNNOTICED AND UNTOUCHED
MARRIAGE BEHIND THE FAÇADE
CAPTIVE BUT FORBIDDEN
STRANGERS IN THE DESERT

Did you know these are also available as eBooks?
Visit www.millsandboon.co.uk

REVELATIONS OF THE NIGHT BEFORE

BY
LYNN RAYE HARRIS

First published in Great Britain 2012
by Mills & Boon, an imprint of Harlequin (UK) Limited.
Harlequin (UK) Limited, Eton House, 18-24 Paradise Road,
Richmond, Surrey TW9 1SR

© Lynn Raye Harris 2012

ISBN: 978 0 263 89122 5

Harlequin (UK) policy is to use papers that are natural, renewable and recyclable products and made from wood grown in sustainable forests. The logging and manufacturing process conform to the legal environmental regulations of the country of origin.

Printed and bound in Spain
by Blackprint CPI, Barcelona

REVELATIONS
OF THE
NIGHT BEFORE

For Beverly Barton.
You left us too soon, and we all miss you tremendously.
Thank you for your kindness, your encouragement and
your enthusiasm. You were what a true Southern lady
should be. Now that you've arrived, I'm sure Heaven is
breaking out the cloth napkins and good china daily.

CHAPTER ONE

SHE could not possibly be pregnant. Valentina D'Angeli's fingers shook as she studied the test stick, the blue line very clearly trying to tell her she was indeed expecting a baby.

It was too crazy to be believed, and yet...

A chill slid down her spine. The night of the masquerade ball had been the wildest she'd ever experienced; the one night where she'd determined to let down her hair and be the person she'd never been able to be. The free spirit who could sleep with a man and leave him in the morning without a shred of remorse.

For one night, she'd planned to be bold and seductive. She *would* experience passion and conquer her shyness once and for all. She *would* be like other women her age—sophisticated, experienced and utterly in control.

Tina set the test stick down and opened another. Surely the first had been damaged somehow. The second would give her the correct answer.

That night had been a good idea in theory, yet even with the anonymity of the mask, she'd been unable to let herself go to the extent her best friend, Lucia, had decided she should.

"You need to get laid, Tina," Lucia had said.

Tina had blushed and stammered and said yes, of

course she needed to—she was tired of being a twenty-four-year-old virgin—but she'd not truly thought it would happen. She'd tried to flirt and dance and be free, but when her partner had pulled her close, his breath smelling faintly of garlic and mint combined, she'd known she couldn't do it. She'd pushed away from him and run from the palazzo, out onto the dock where it had been quieter and cooler, and gulped in the Venetian night air like a balm.

And that's when he'd appeared. Not the man she'd run from, but the man she would give herself to before the night was over. He'd been tall, suave, dressed in black velvet and wearing a silk mask over his eyes.

He'd been utterly mesmerizing, and she'd fallen under his spell with far more ease than she'd ever expected. He'd made love to her so tenderly, so perfectly, that she'd wept with the beauty of it.

And with the loneliness of it.

"No names," he'd whispered in her ear. "No faces."

She'd agreed, because that was what had made it magical—and yet, once it was over, she'd wanted to know him. She'd felt bereft with the idea she never would.

Tina swallowed the fear that rose from the pit of her stomach and grabbed her by the throat. Sometimes, not knowing was the best thing. She wished to God she still didn't know.

But as the light from the full moon had slid between the curtains and illuminated the sleeping form of the man beside her, she'd dared to slide the silk mask from his eyes. Her breath stopped in her chest just remembering that moment.

He hadn't awakened, even when she'd gasped. Even when she'd scrambled from the bed and stood there in the quiet, elegant bedroom of the hotel he'd taken her to. Her heart had turned over, her stomach flipping inside out.

Of all the men in the world.

She'd reacted blindly then. She'd yanked on her clothes as silently as she could—and then she'd fled like the coward she was.

"Right," she said to herself as she waited for the new test stick to negate the first one. The universe was simply playing a huge joke on her, punishing her for that night of wanton behavior with a man she should not have known at all. What kind of woman gave herself to a man she didn't even know?

But you do know him. You've always known him. Always wanted him.

Tina chewed her lip, her heart beating erratically as the seconds ticked by.

And then the answer came, as clear and soul shattering as the first.

Pregnant.

"There is a woman, my lord," the man said apologetically.

Niccolo Gavretti, the marchese di Casari, turned from where he'd been gazing out the window of the exclusive Roman hotel's restaurant and fixed the maître d' with an even look.

There was always a woman. Women were his favorite hobby—when they weren't demanding more than he was willing to give or thinking that because he'd slept with them, he owed them something more.

No, he loved women—but on his terms.

"Where is this woman then," he asked almost wearily.

"She refuses to come inside, my lord." His tone said that he did not approve.

Nico waived a hand dismissively. "Then she is not my problem."

The maître d' bowed. "As you wish, my lord."

Nico turned back to his paper. He'd come here this morning for a business breakfast with an associate, but he'd stayed to drink coffee and read the paper once the meeting was over. He'd not expected a woman to accost him, but then he was hardly surprised, either. A determined woman was often a force to be reckoned with.

Sometimes the results were quite pleasurable and interesting. Other times, not so much.

Only a few moments passed before the maître d' returned, apologetic and red-faced. "My lord, I beg your pardon."

Nico set the paper down. His patience was running thin. He had much on his mind lately, not the least of which was dealing with the vast mess his father had bequeathed to him.

"Yes, Andres?"

"The lady says it is most urgent that she speak to you. But she cannot do so in such a public place. She suggests you come to her room."

Nico resisted rolling his eyes, but only just. Before his father's death, Nico had been one of the top-ranked Grand Prix motorcycle riders in the world. He'd won the world championship a few months ago. He knew all about the kinds of schemes a woman might employ to catch his interest. He had been the object of many such plots in his life. Sometimes he played along because it amused him to do so.

Today would not be one of those times.

"Please tell her she will be waiting for a very long

time," he said smoothly. And then he glanced at his watch. "I have an appointment elsewhere, I'm afraid."

The maître d's face was a study in contrasts. He looked simultaneously uncomfortable and...*gleeful* was the word Nico wanted...all at once. "She said if you refused to give you this, my lord."

He held out an envelope on a small tray. Nico hesitated, furious to be playing this game—and intrigued, damn him, as well. He jerked the envelope from the tray and ripped it open. A business card fell out. It was white, plain, with only a stylized *D* in one corner.

It was the name on the card that pierced him to the bone. He stared at the sweeping font that separated the two words from the paper.

Valentina D'Angeli.

The name sent a slice of old anger ricocheting through him. Not the first name; the last. Valentina's brother, Renzo D'Angeli, had been his greatest rival on the track. His greatest rival in business, even now.

But once, Renzo had been his best friend. Nico and Renzo had worked together building a motorcycle that would take the racing world by storm—until everything had fallen apart amid accusations of betrayal and deceit.

It was a long time ago, and yet it still had the power to make Nico's blood hum with dangerous anger. And sadness.

He focused on the name, tried to remember the girl who'd still been a teenager the last time he'd seen her. Valentina D'Angeli. She would be all grown up now. Twenty-four, he calculated. He'd not seen her since the day he'd walked away from the D'Angelis' house for the last time, knowing he would never be welcomed back again.

Valentina had been a sweet girl, but terribly shy. Her

shyness, he remembered, had bothered her brother. So much so that Renzo had planned to send her away to school once he had the money to do so, in the hopes that an exclusive education could fix her.

Nico had tried to convince Renzo to reconsider. He knew what it was like to be sent away to school, and he'd not been shy in the least. He'd felt isolated, no matter how many friends he'd had or how well he'd done in class. And he'd hated the loneliness, the feeling that his parents were happier without him, and that he was in the way when he was at home.

Nico frowned. It hadn't been far from the truth, but he hadn't found that out until a few years later.

Still, the exclusive education had certainly done its work on him. He had no doubt that it had done its work on Valentina, as well. The raw stone would now be polished to a high shine.

But what was she doing here?

Nico turned the card over. *Room 386* was written on the back. He closed his hand over it. He should walk away. He should get up and walk out the door and forget he'd ever seen this card.

But he wouldn't. He wanted to know what she wanted from him. Renzo must have sent her, but for what purpose? He'd not seen Renzo since that day on the track in Dubai, the first race of the Grand Prix circuit. Renzo had walked away from racing after it was over. He'd married his secretary and was currently making babies in the country, according to everything Nico had heard.

His blood ran cold. Renzo might be done racing, but he wasn't done with motorcycles. They were still rivals in business. And Renzo must want something pretty badly to send his sister to get it.

* * *

She was nervous. Tina stood by the window and watched the cars moving along the street below. She did not know if he would come. What if he didn't? Did she dare to go to his offices and demand to be seen? Or should she try and see him at his country estate instead?

Except he had more than one country estate these days, didn't he? It had been nearly two months since she'd seen him in Venice. In that short time, his father had died and Nico was now the marchese di Casari, a man of far more consequence than he'd been when he used to spend hours working in the garage with Renzo.

Would a man of his stature come to see her? He and Renzo had been enemies for far longer than they'd ever been friends. It was very likely that Nico remembered nothing of her. She'd been a gangly girl, quiet and shy, who had crept into the garage and watched them silently. She hadn't been at all memorable.

But that was a lifetime ago, and now she stood here pregnant with his child. Tina sucked in a tearful breath. My God. How—*how*—had this happened? It had been one night, one erotic and beautiful night in which she'd behaved in a way so very unlike her.

She'd hated being so shy growing up, hated even more that no matter how much education she'd had or how hard she worked at being someone bold and sophisticated, she was still the same painfully timid girl inside. The one time she'd determined to push past her comfort zone, to *really* be bold, the consequences had been staggering.

If she'd known who her mystery man was, she would have fled sooner. Because she wouldn't have been able to let herself go so thoroughly if she'd known that the man stripping her naked was the same man she'd dreamed about for most of her life.

When she was fourteen, she'd idolized him. He'd been twenty and so achingly handsome that he'd taken her breath away. She'd never learned to relax around him even though he was always nice to her. He'd smiled at her, and she'd turned into a stammering puddle every single time.

And then one day when she'd crept into the garage just to see his handsome face, he hadn't been there. He'd never been there again, and Renzo had refused to talk about it. She'd lain in her room at night for months and prayed he would come back, but he never did.

There was a knock on the door and Tina jumped at the sound like a startled deer. Doubts assailed her. Should she even be here? Should she tell him her secret?

He would be furious. And quite possibly horrified.

But how could she not? He had a right to know he was going to be a father. A right to know his baby. She'd never known her own father and her mother had refused to tell her who he was, other than to say he'd been English. She would not do that to her own child, no matter how difficult this was.

Swiftly, she strode to the door and yanked it open before she could change her mind. The man on the threshold was tall, dark, gorgeous—a more mature version of the young man she'd fallen for so many years ago. Just seeing him again made sparks zing through her body.

He simmered with tension as his stormy gaze met hers. And then he dropped his eyes down her body, studying her so thoroughly that she blushed.

She'd chosen to wear a skirt with sky-high heels and a silk tank beneath her jacket for this meeting. She knew she looked elegant and competent, as she'd intended, but for a moment the hideously shy teenager was back.

"Valentina?" he said, his voice containing a note

of disbelief, and a hint of that sexual magnetism she'd found so irresistible in Venice. How had she forgotten his voice over the years? She could have avoided the situation she was now in if she'd only remembered the silken beauty of his tone, and recognized him sooner.

"Yes. It's lovely to see you again, Signore Gavretti." She stepped back, her heart pushing into her throat. She'd spent a night of bliss in his arms, and he had no idea. Until that very moment, she'd half believed he would recognize her when he saw her. That somehow his soul would know she was the one he'd made love to.

But he did not, and it pierced her to the bone. *Silly.* He was a man, not a magician.

"Won't you come in?"

He crossed the threshold, and for a moment an invisible hand closed around her throat. What had she done? Why had she thought she could handle him? She'd been unable to handle him that night. No, she'd done everything he'd wanted her to do. Willingly, eagerly, thoroughly—as if the shyness she hid from the world had ceased to exist.

Her body heated as the memories rushed through her. Skin against skin, heat against heat, hard against soft. What would he think of her when he knew?

Tina shoved the memories down deep and walked over to a serving cart. "Tea?" she asked, her hand shaking slightly as she reached for the pot. What she really wanted to do was grab a plate and fan herself with it.

"No."

She poured herself a cup—decaf, of course—and turned to find him right behind her. She took an automatic step back. His stormy silver eyes were piercing, his expression hard and curious at once. She wanted to run her hand over his jaw, press her lips there the way she had that night…which seemed a lifetime ago.

"You didn't ask me up here to have tea," he said darkly. "Tell me what your brother wants and be done with it."

Tina blinked, the warm feelings floating through her dissipating in an instant. "Renzo has no idea I'm here." God, no. He'd be furious. Livid. He would probably disown her if he knew.

And he would know, eventually. But that was why she had to tell Nico first. If Renzo found out she were pregnant, he would demand to know the father. There would be hell to pay once he knew who that man was.

Tina set the tea down and pressed a hand to her forehead. It was a mess. A huge, huge mess. Somehow, she had to make it all come out right.

Nico's smile was anything but friendly. "So this is how we are to play it then?" His gaze slid over her again. "You have grown into a lovely woman, Valentina. A great asset for your brother."

Tina wanted to laugh, but she couldn't. She couldn't show that much vulnerability to him. No, Renzo did not consider her an asset. More like a duty. He took care of her, loved her, but refused to consider she might have more to offer than simply being a decorative fixture in his life. She wanted to work for him, but he would not allow it.

"You are a D'Angeli," he said. *"You don't have to work."*

No, she didn't have to work. She *wanted* to work— and if her brother wouldn't hire her, she was going to work for someone else. She'd gone along with Renzo for the past year, but only in the hopes she could convince him that D'Angeli Motors was where she belonged.

Though she'd graduated with honors in accounting and finance, the only thing she could do with her degree right now, aside from dabble in a few investments with the payouts from her trust fund, was balance her own checkbook.

It made her waspish. "You can hardly claim to know what is in Renzo's mind these days, can you?"

He stared at her for a heartbeat, his expression hardening. She'd surprised herself by being so snappish. Apparently, she'd surprised him, too.

"Enough of the games. Tell me why you requested this meeting, or we're through here."

His tone stung. "You did not used to be so abrupt."

"And you did not used to play games."

Tina carried her tea to the couch. She sat gracefully as she'd been taught, and then took a tiny sip, hoping it would calm her suddenly roiling stomach. Perhaps she'd erred in not eating breakfast this morning. But she'd taken one look at the meats, cheeses and eggs arrayed before her on the table and felt she would be violently ill if she ate a bite.

"I'm not playing a game, *signore*. I'm just unsure how to begin this." It was the truth.

"You used to call me Nico," he said. "When you managed to speak to me at all."

She felt herself flushing with embarrassment at the memory of how she used to be so tongue-tied around him. His face was stern and foreboding, his body tense as he loomed over her in his expensive suit and studied her as if she were something he'd stepped in.

If only he knew…

Tina had to suppress a wild giggle. It wasn't amusement so much as hysteria, but nevertheless she could hardly give in to it. Besides, he would know soon enough, wouldn't he? Just as soon as she could manage to say the words.

"That was a long time ago," she said. "Life was simpler then."

She thought a flash of emotion crossed his features, but it was gone as suddenly as it had appeared. "Life is never simple, *cara*. It only seems so in retrospect."

"What happened between you and Renzo?" The words fell from her lips, though she did not intend for them to. Any softening she might have seen on his face was gone again.

"We ceased to be friends. That is enough."

Tina sighed. She'd always wanted to know why he'd stopped coming around, but Renzo remained tight-lipped about the whole thing. She'd been too young to really understand back then, but she'd thought it was probably temporary. A disagreement between friends.

She'd been wrong.

Her stomach clenched again and she splayed her hand over her belly, as if she could stop the churning simply by doing so.

Nico was on one knee in front of her suddenly. His eyes were the color of a leaden sky, she thought wildly. Any minute the storm would break. Any minute.

But for now he looked concerned, and her heart squeezed. "What is the matter, Valentina? You look… green."

She swallowed the bile that threatened and tried to sip the tea again. "I'm pregnant," she said, her heart beating in her ears, her throat.

"Congratulations." It was said sincerely. And it was all she could do to hold in the nervous laughter pressing at the back of her throat.

"Thank you." She felt hot, so hot. She could feel the

sweat beading on her forehead, her upper lip. She set the tea down and peeled the jacket from her shoulders. Nico reached up to help her. He stood and laid the jacket over the back of the couch.

His expression was gentler now, but he was still like a caged lion roaming the quiet space of the suite. Any second, and his fangs would be bared, his claws extended.

Tina closed her eyes and shook her head slightly. *Focus.*

"Can I get you anything?" he asked.

"One of those biscuits would be nice," she said.

He retrieved a vanilla biscuit from the tea table and handed it to her. Tina broke off a piece and chewed slowly.

Nico shoved his hands in his pockets. "If you could state your business, we can solve whatever this is and go our separate ways."

"Yes, I suppose we can." Would he want to be involved? Or would he wash his hands of her the moment she told him? It didn't really matter, she decided. She was strong enough to have this baby on her own. No one was going to stop her from doing so, either.

She finished the biscuit and leaned back on the couch. It seemed the food would stay down this time, but she knew she needed to eat more.

"I had not realized you'd married," Nico said.

Her gaze snapped to his, her pulse thrumming. "I'm not married."

His pause was significant. "Ah."

Tina fumed at the unspoken implications. "I did not plan this, but I won't be ashamed of my baby, either."

"I did not say you should be." And yet she did not believe him. People like him—people who came from families like his—had very stringent views on proper behavior. She'd learned that in boarding school when the other girls had treated her like scum for not having a father. For having a mother who had once been a waitress, and who had never married even though she'd had children.

Those girls had made her life hell at St. Katherine's. They hated her because she hadn't been from old money, because she'd been shy and an easy target for their venom. Rotten snobs, all of them. Except Lucia, of course.

Tina clenched her fingers into the cushion. Nico was one of those people, from old money and lineage. And he was judging her, finding her lacking. It should make her want to hide.

Instead, it made her angry. "No, you did not say anything. But you're thinking it."

He looked cool and gorgeous standing there. Remote. "I'm not thinking anything. Except for what any of this possibly has to do with me."

She stared at him for several heartbeats, as her breath seemed to stop inside her lungs. It was now or never, wasn't it? He'd given her the opportunity. She had to say the words. But forcing them out was like trying to stop snowflakes from melting on her tongue.

"It has everything to do with you," she finally managed, her voice little more than a whisper.

But he heard her. His expression changed, became even icier. He was the aristocrat, and she was the mixed breed dog who didn't even have a father.

"I fail to see how. Until today, I haven't laid eyes on you in nearly ten years. And believe me," he said, his gaze skimming over her again, "I would remember doing so."

His voice was sex itself, and she flushed. But she

looked him dead in the eye and refused to flinch as she said the next words.

"Not necessarily. Not if it was dark and we—we wore masks."

CHAPTER TWO

NICO's stomach felt strangely hollow. He was standing here, looking at this woman who he could hardly believe was the grown-up little sister of his old friend and archrival, and he knew what she was saying even though she did not actually speak the words.

She was telling him she was pregnant. With his child.

But he knew it was a lie. No matter what she said about Venice and the masks, she was not that woman. It was a trick, a ruse cooked up by her brother in order to settle old scores. Oddly, it disappointed him to think she could be as ruthless as Renzo when she'd once been so shy.

He didn't know how they knew, but he would not fall for it.

His gaze raked her body as he tried to recall the woman he'd shared that night with. He'd found her on the docks outside the palazzo, gulping air and shivering. He'd feared something bad had happened to her initially, but that had not been the case at all.

He remembered how sweetly innocent she'd been, and how he'd been drawn to her in spite of his usual preference for more experienced bed partners. He had not thought she would be a virgin, but she'd surprised him on that score, as well.

How could this be the same woman?

It couldn't be. Somehow, Valentina D'Angeli knew the woman he'd been with and she and her brother were using the situation to their advantage. It was too outrageous otherwise.

"You are lying," he said.

Her eyes widened with hurt. "Why would I do that? What could I possibly gain from something like this?"

Fury roared through him in giant waves. She played the innocent so well. "I can imagine a few things," he grated. "I am wealthy. Titled. And my company is a thorn in D'Angeli Motors' side."

Her brows drew down in a dark frown. Unwelcome heat flared inside him as she stood.

It hit him like a blow that she was very beautiful, with strong features and smooth skin and a mouth that needed kissing. Her chestnut hair tumbled over her shoulders in an insane riot of curls. He would have remembered hair like that, hair that twisted and curled and caught the light like it had been dusted with gold. He cast his mind back to that night, saw long dark hair that was thick and shiny…and straight.

Violet eyes flashed fire as she put her hands on her hips and faced him squarely. "Six weeks ago, you did not have a title. And my brother has as much money as you do, if not more. As for the companies, I could give a damn about either of them for all the good it would do me."

Nico tried not to be distracted by the way her waist curved in over the flare of her hips or the way her posture emphasized the full thrust of her breasts against her silk shirt. His body was hyperaware of her, but he could handle that. He simply refused to give in to the attraction.

"Her hair was straight," he said coldly.

She blinked, and triumph surged within him. He had her there. What a pretty liar she was.

Then she laughed at him as she twisted a finger into a curl and pulled it straight. "It's called a blow out, you idiot. Give me twenty minutes with a hair dryer, and I'll show you hair as straight as a file."

He stiffened. "That hardly proves it was you."

She took a step closer to him, and he had the distinct impression she was stalking him. It turned him on more than it ought. For a moment he wanted to close the distance between them, wanted to fit his mouth to hers and see if the sparks he felt in the air also extended to the physical. He had enough self-control not to do so, however.

She tilted her chin up, those eyes still flashing fire at him. She had a temper. He didn't remember that about her, but then she'd only been a teenager when he'd last known her. All he remembered about her then was a girl who hid behind her hair and went mute whenever he spoke to her.

Now she jabbed a manicured finger at him. "Shall I tell you everything about that night, starting with the moment you asked me if I was okay on the dock? Or should I describe your room at the Hotel Daniele? The way you turned off all the lights and told me no names and no faces? The way you peeled off my gown and kissed my skin while I—" here she swallowed "—I gasped?"

She broke off then, her face red, and Nico felt a jolt of need coiling at the base of his spine. He'd bedded a lot of women over the years, but none so fascinating as the one he'd taken that night. It had been a true one-night stand, and in the morning he'd awakened to find her gone. He'd been rather amused with the way it had made him feel, as if she'd used him and discarded him, and yet he'd been wistful, too.

Because, no matter what he'd said to his mystery woman about remaining anonymous, he'd wanted to see her again after that night. There'd been something between them that he'd wanted to explore further. It had only been sex, he knew that, but when he found a woman he enjoyed, he usually spent more than one night with her.

He'd asked the hotel staff if they remembered her or if they had seen which direction she'd gone in when she'd left.

The lone man on duty that night had said she'd left around two in the morning, silk-and-feather mask intact and pale green dress clutched in her fists as she ran through the lobby. He had not noted which direction she'd gone after she'd taken the gondola, and he didn't remember which gondolier had taken her.

A general inquiry of the gondoliers plying that part of the city had turned up nothing.

And that had been the end of that. Nico had been disappointed, but he'd gotten over it soon enough. It was sex, not love—and he could find plenty of sexual partners when the need arose. One sexy, inexperienced woman was not necessary to his life any more than a fine brandy was. They were both enjoyable, but completely dispensable.

"You could have learned those details from someone else. They prove nothing," he told her. And yet his blood hummed at her nearness, almost the way it had that night.

Her head dipped then, her eyes dropping away from his. "This is ridiculous," she breathed. And then she turned and sank onto the couch again, her eyes closing as her skin whitened.

Guilt pricked him. "Do you need another biscuit? More tea?"

"No. I just need to sit a moment." She looked up at him, her mouth turning down in a frown. "You're right, of course. I'm making the whole thing up. Renzo put me up to it so we could embarrass you. Because of course you would be embarrassed, wouldn't you? You, the man who has at least a dozen scantily clad paddock girls clinging to you after your races, the man who appears in the tabloids on a regular basis with some new woman on his arm, the man who famously stood in the middle of a party one evening and kissed every woman who asked to be kissed—yes, that man would be so embarrassed by me and my baby, though we would probably only burnish his bad-boy reputation."

Anger flared inside him. She was making fun of him—and the worst part was that what she said made a perverse sort of sense.

"How do I know what you and Renzo have in mind?" he snapped. "Perhaps you see this as a way to infuse the D'Angeli blood with legitimacy and credibility. This isn't the first time I've had to deal with title hunters, and I'm sure it won't be the last."

He didn't think it was possible she could grow any paler, but she did.

"You are vile," she said. "So full of yourself and your inflated sense of self-importance. I don't know why I wanted to tell you about the baby, but I thought you had a right to know. And I *certainly* don't want anything from you. Now, if you don't mind, I'd like to just sit here quietly. I'd show you out, but I'm certain you can find the door."

Nico stared down at her for several heartbeats. She seemed distressed, and his natural instinct was to stay and help her. But he couldn't forgive what she was trying to do to him.

"You've forgotten one very important detail about that night, *cara.* Perhaps your informant failed to mention it, or perhaps she did and you were hoping I'd forgotten, but we used protection. I may enjoy a variety of bed partners, but I am not stupid or careless."

"I'm well aware of it, but the box does say ninety-nine percent effective, does it not? We seem to be the one percent for whom it was not."

His jaw clenched together so hard he thought his teeth might crack. "Nice try, *bella,* but it's not working. Tell Renzo to think up something else."

And then he walked out the door and shut it firmly behind him.

Tina wanted to throw something, but the effort wouldn't be worth the slim satisfaction she would feel, so she continued to sit on the couch, sip tea and nibble biscuits until her stomach calmed down.

She should feel satisfied that she'd done the right thing and told him, but all she felt was anger and frustration. Whatever had happened between her brother and Nico, it had certainly created a lingering animosity.

She had come to a realization, though. She would not tell Renzo who had fathered her baby. He would demand to know, but it wasn't his right to know. She was twenty-four and capable of making her own decisions. She'd gotten herself into this, and she would deal with the consequences. Perhaps it was for the best that Nico refused to believe her. Now it wasn't necessary that she tell anyone.

Her mother, at least, would support her decision. How could she not, when she'd spent years denying Tina the right to know who her own father was?

Tina frowned. Poor Mama. Her mother had been in and out of love dozens of times that Tina could recall. Even now, she was off to Bora-Bora with her current lover, a man who Tina hoped was finally the right one. If anyone deserved love, it was Mama. She'd worked hard and sacrificed a lot until Renzo had started building his motorcycles and making money at it.

Tina sighed. At least she had a reprieve for a while. Mama was away, and Renzo, Faith and their baby were on their private yacht somewhere in the Caribbean, enjoying their first vacation in months. Not only that, but Renzo was also recuperating from surgery to repair his damaged leg. The last thing she wanted was to disrupt his recovery with her news.

No, as much as she might like to talk to her sister-in-law about being pregnant, Tina knew it was best if she was alone for now. By the time everyone returned, she would be further along and more confident in her ability to deal with them all.

As the afternoon wore on, she started to feel immensely better. She decided to leave Rome early the next morning and head for the family vacation home on Capri. She felt jittery after her meeting with Nico and she wanted to get far away from the city. From him. Not that she expected him to come back, but knowing he was in the same city—sleeping, eating, having sex with other women—was too much just now.

A few days in the lemon-scented breezes of Capri would do her good. But first she would call Lucia and see if her friend wanted to get together for dinner. She hadn't yet told anyone she was pregnant; she would start with Lucia, see how that went. If nothing else, it would be good practice for that moment when she had to tell her family.

Tina had not told Lucia who her mystery lover had been, though she'd admitted to spending the night with a man when Lucia had pressed her about it. Her friend had been so happy to hear it, as if she'd never quite believed that Tina would go through with it.

Tina wasn't sure Lucia would be happy about the consequences, however.

She left a message on Lucia's mobile phone and then decided to go to the Via dei Condotti for some shopping. But first she would walk from the Piazza Navona to the Pantheon in order to clear her head a bit. The walk wasn't long, but it wound through some of the most picturesque of Rome's neighborhoods. She changed into jeans and sandals and added a scarf around her neck.

When she was done, she left the hotel and headed for the Pantheon. She passed gelato shops, antiques shops with paintings and elegant inlaid furniture in the windows, trattorias with chairs and tables lining the pedestrian way, and finally came out on the square where the Pantheon sat, ancient and silent against a bright blue sky.

It was her favorite monument in Rome. She passed inside, beneath the forest of tall columns and into the cavernous chamber with the huge circle cut out in the center of the ceiling high above. Ignoring the tourists with their cameras, she skirted the roped off area in the center and took a seat on one of the benches facing the altar that had been added much later when the structure had been turned into a church.

And then she tilted her head back and watched a wisp of a cloud float over the opening above. For some reason, this building made her feel peaceful. It always had. Once, when she had been home on break from school and didn't want to go back again, she'd snuck out of Renzo's apartment and come here. She'd sat for hours just like this until one of her brother's security team had found her and made her return home and, ultimately, back to the private school that had terrified her until she'd met Lucia and made a friend.

"She had a scar." The voice in her ear was startling. The noise in the Pantheon was always a dull murmur, but this voice pierced her solitude and made her gasp.

Tina whipped around to look at the dark, brooding male now sitting beside her on the bench. Her heart flipped, as it always did, whenever she looked at him. It was very annoying.

"An appendix scar," he continued. "Just here." He made a slashing motion over his abdomen, to the right of his belly button and above his hip bone.

"I had my appendix out four years ago," she said coolly.

His silver eyes looked troubled. "I don't suppose you would show me this scar?"

"I would, in fact. But not at this very moment, if you don't mind. And even if you do," she added irritably. She would not jump to his tune just because he wished it.

The intensity of his gaze did not relent. "Assuming you have this scar, and you are the woman from that night, how did you know it was me?"

She looked up at the perfectly round slice of sky overhead. A bird sailed high over the opening, wings outstretched as it rode the currents. "I slid your mask off. And when I realized who you were, I ran away."

"How do I know that's the truth? That you didn't wait for me that night and set the whole thing up?"

She turned her head to meet his hot gaze, and her belly clenched. It was a different sensation than the one where the baby played havoc with her body. This tightening was a feeling that happened whenever she looked at this man. Only at this man. It was startling and disturbing all at once.

"Don't you suppose that if I'd been waiting for you, I'd have gone about the whole thing differently? I'm pretty sure that hiding on the dock like a frightened, nearly sick child isn't exactly the way to attract a man."

"And yet it worked," he said coldly.

Tina sat up straight, fury vibrating through her. "Look, if you want to believe this is all a ruse, that I'm lying or that I set you up, then fine, believe it. But don't sit here and bother me with your theories, okay? I told you what I thought you should know, and now I'm done. I don't want anything from you, Nico. I don't expect anything. I just thought you might like to know your child."

She started to rise, but he clamped a hand around her wrist and kept her on the bench. His fingers were long and strong, and his touch sent a jolt of energy radiating through her body. She jerked her wrist away and folded her arms over her midsection.

He bent closer to her until only she could hear the hard words coming from his lips. "*If* you are carrying my child, Valentina, I will be involved in his life. I refuse to pay child support and only see him whenever you allow it, or whenever the courts dictate. If you are carrying my child, then *you* are mine, as well."

His eyes were stormy gray pools that slid deep into her soul and tore at her facade of calm. Her instinct was to recoil, but she didn't. She hadn't lived through boarding school, and the blue-blooded girls—girls from families like his—who'd thought they were far better than she was, to cave in whenever a man glared at her and told her how he believed things were going to be done.

When met with icy disdain, she returned icy disdain.

She shouldered her purse and stood. This time he did not try to stop her. It was a comfort to be able to gaze down at him, but she realized it was a false comfort. He was as dangerous as always, as tightly leashed and volatile as a stick of dynamite.

And she was about to light the fuse.

"You don't own me, Nico. If you want to be involved, we'll work something out. I want our baby to know his—or *her*—father. You both deserve that. And I want you to be in our baby's life. But I won't be part of the game between you and Renzo. I refuse to be."

The fuse sparked and caught. His smile was cold and lethal, and she shivered deep inside. He lived for this, she thought. Lived for mayhem and challenge. It was why he rode the motorcycles at death-defying speeds, why he slept his way through the phone book without remorse, and why he was not about to back down now.

She'd lit the fuse, but the explosion would be a long time coming. And it frightened her.

"Too late, *cara*," he said silkily. "You already are."

CHAPTER THREE

THEY sat inside a hotel restaurant facing the Pantheon and Tina stared at the crowds milling in the square. People with cameras, backpacks and books strolled around with their chins in the air, their necks craned to take in the ancient structure. A horse and carriage sat nearby, waiting to take tourists willing to part with their money on a short ride to the next attraction.

They looked happy, she thought wistfully. Happy people seeing the sights while she sat inside the crowded hotel at a table beside the window and waited for someone to bring her a bowl of soup.

Nico sat across from her, his big body sprawled elegantly in the chair, his phone to his ear. She'd tried to walk out on him, but she'd not gotten far before she'd had to stop and lean against a column for a moment.

And he was there, his fingers closing around her arm, holding her up, pulling her into the curve of his body. Then he'd demanded to know what she'd eaten that day. When she'd said only a biscuit or two, he'd hauled her over to this restaurant and plunked her down at the table before ordering soup, bread and *acqua minerale*.

He finished his call and picked up his coffee in a long-fingered hand while she resolutely looked away. She didn't want to study the beauty of those fingers, didn't want to remember them on her body, the way they'd stroked her so softly and sensually, the way they'd awakened sensations inside her that she'd never quite felt before.

Everything about being with Nico had been a revelation. As much as she wished she could forget the whole thing, she could in fact forget nothing. Worse, she wanted to experience it all again.

The soup arrived and she found that she was starving. After a few careful bites, she ate with more gusto than she'd been able to enjoy for days now. She didn't know if the soup would stay down, but eating was preferable to talking to Nico right now.

She could feel him watching her. Finally, she looked up and caught him studying her as if he were really seeing her for the first time. It disconcerted her.

She dropped the spoon and sat back. "Is there a problem?" she snapped. The words shocked her since she didn't usually seek confrontation as she couldn't bear to have anyone angry with her.

And yet she found she did not care when it came to this man. He was already angry with her. What did it matter if she challenged him? It would change nothing about the way he sat there smoldering with fury.

And blistering sex appeal. She couldn't forget the sex appeal.

"Nothing I can't handle," he said smoothly, and she felt angry color rising in her cheeks. He was baiting her and she was falling for it every time. Why couldn't she just keep her mouth shut and let him smolder?

Hard on the heels of anger came fear. It surprised her. But it was a cold fear that wrapped around her throat and squeezed as she considered all the implications of what had happened between them.

Why had she told him about the baby? She should have kept silent. It wouldn't have truly hurt her baby not to know its father just as it hadn't hurt her. And her family would be safe from this man's fury.

Because he was furious, she was certain. Coldly furious. And calculating. She had no idea what he was capable of, but she feared it. He was not the same person he'd been when she'd idolized him as a teen.

"I appreciate the lunch," she said, pushing her chair back, "but I'm afraid I have to go now."

He watched her almost indolently. She wasn't fooled. He was like a great cat lounging in the sun, one minute content, the next springing to life to bring down a gazelle.

"You aren't going anywhere, Valentina." He spoke mildly, but again she was reminded of the cat. He was toying with her.

She thrust her chin out. "You can't stop me."

His eyes gleamed in the light streaming in from the window. "I already have." He motioned to the waiter, and then took out a credit card and handed it to the man when he arrived with the bill.

Tina sucked in a deep breath and tried not to panic. She was not this man's prisoner. She could get up and walk out of this restaurant and there was nothing he could do to stop her. He didn't own her in any way, nor would he.

Tina grabbed her purse and headed for the exit. She didn't run, but she was very aware of what was happening behind her. Nico didn't say a word, his chair didn't scrape the floor, and she breathed a sigh of relief that he wasn't following her. She burst into the open, the sunlight lasering into her eyes as the noise from the square assaulted her.

She turned and walked blindly, not caring where she went so long as Nico did not follow. This time, she would escape him. She would return to the hotel soon enough, but for now she just wanted to get lost in the crowds. He did not own her, no matter what he said. She repeated it over and over to herself as she walked down the cobbled streets, dodging tourists with cameras who weren't paying attention to where they were going, and men who hooted and whistled at her.

These were not the middle ages; women had babies on their own all the time. She did not need a man in her life, and she certainly didn't need that one. He could not compel her to do anything she did not want to do.

Tina walked until she found herself crossing a busy street, and then she was among the pedestrians again, walking alongside booths that had designer knock-off purses, scarves, bottle openers, and miniature Colosseums and Pantheons among their wares. The pedestrian traffic grew heavier the farther she went, and then the sound of rushing water came to her ears. A few steps more and she stood in front of the massive facade of the Trevi Fountain. She clutched her purse tightly to her body as she navigated the crowd and made her way down to the foot of the fountain.

Water gushed from below the feet of Neptune, over the troughs below the horses, and into the vast bowl of the fountain. Tina stood there with her heart aching. People laughed and took pictures of each other. A smiling couple held hands and then threw a coin into the water together. Impulsively, Tina dug a coin from her purse and gripped it hard enough so that the smooth round edge imprinted into her palm. Then she closed her eyes and said her wish to herself before she threw it into the water.

She wished that Nico would leave her alone, and that Renzo would never find out who had fathered her baby. *Too late*, a voice in her head told her. *If you'd wanted that, you never should have told him.*

She stood there a few minutes more before she turned to climb back up the steps as people jostled for position. She came to an abrupt stop when she looked up and realized who stood at the top, waiting for her.

So much for wishes.

He was silhouetted against the purpling sky, his dark form drawing more eyes than just hers. Tina's heart skipped a beat as she gazed up into that beautiful dark face. His hands were in his pockets. He looked, for the barest of moments, *lonely*.

But that could not be right. Niccolo Gavretti was not the kind of man who would ever be lonely. He was wealthy, titled and gorgeous. And, as she knew from experience, a sensual and amazing lover.

He was the last person in the world who should ever be lonely.

He held out a hand to her, beckoning her. She took the last few steps, reluctantly placing her hand in his as she neared the top. He steadied her over the last step and then she was standing beside him, her purse clasped to her chest like a shield.

As if anything could protect her from him.

"I've made an appointment with one of the city's top obstetricians, unless you have a doctor you prefer."

She shook her head, suddenly defeated. If she ran, he would follow, and if she fought, he would fight back. He was a force to be reckoned with, and she did not truly want to fight him. That was not how she wished her relationship with the father of her baby to be. If she had a hope of staving off trouble, she would go with him. For now.

Nico put a hand in her back and guided her through the crowd until they popped out onto a street nearby. A dark Mercedes sat with the engine idling, and when they approached it a man got out and opened the door for them.

Once they were inside, the doors closed and they were soon moving through traffic. The glass was up between the driver and them, and there was nothing but silence in the rich interior of the car.

"Now would be a good time to show me the scar," Nico said at last.

"I'm not sure I want to," she said softly. "I think I liked it better when you thought I was lying."

The leather squeaked as he turned toward her. "I'm not going to hurt you, Valentina."

"Or my family," she added firmly. Because she realized now that it was a very real possibility he would go after Renzo somehow. She had seriously underestimated the depth of his hatred for her brother—and Renzo's for him.

There was silence for a moment. "I can't promise that."

Her heart felt pinched in her chest. She pictured Renzo with Faith and their son, and it killed her to think that she could be responsible for causing them trouble. "I will do as you ask, without complaint, so long as you leave Renzo out of this."

He studied her for a long moment. "I'm still not positive he doesn't have something to do with this situation. Why would I leave him out of it?"

This is your fault.

Yes, it was her fault. Anger began to swell inside her

again, crowding out the despair, glowing and expanding until she thought she would burst with it, until her skin was on fire from trying to contain it all. *Men!*

"I love my brother, but if you think for one moment I would agree to some scheme that involved me getting pregnant just so he could get back at you somehow, then you *are* insane! What woman in her right mind would let her body be used like that for the express purpose of revenge? I have no idea what happened between you, but no one died so I'm pretty certain it wasn't that bad. What you're suggesting is disgusting.

"And not only that," she added when he didn't say anything, "I think the two of you are pigheaded and foolish for allowing this to continue all these years. It's childish to have a *mortal enemy*. No one has mortal enemies these days."

"Rich men do," he said, but for once his voice wasn't harsh or hard or angry.

Tina folded her arms against her body. "I doubt it's that bad. I simply think you make it so."

"What an innocent life you've led," he replied, and a current of old shame flooded her.

Yes, she'd been naive for far too long. She'd grown up sheltered, pampered and scared to say boo. Boarding school, and then university, had done much to erode her shyness—but at heart she was still that girl who hid behind her hair and feared the world.

Except that she refused to show that fear. To anyone. She put a hand over her belly. She had to be strong now, no matter what. No matter that she was scared. No matter that she quaked inside at the thought of what she'd done to her family.

"If by 'innocent' you mean that I fail to see the need to harm others, then fine, call me innocent."

He made a soft noise of disbelief. "In business, my dear, you must always be willing to be ruthless. It's the only way to survive and thrive."

"And yet it's not necessary in one's personal life, is it? Any man who is ruthless in his personal life will soon find himself alone."

"Perhaps it's not so bad to be alone," he said. "Able to choose when you share your life and bed with someone, and able to go home again when you're tired of the work that being with another person takes."

"It sounds like an empty life," she said sadly.

His jaw tightened only slightly, but she knew she'd scored a hit. What she didn't know was why. She'd spent the past few years reading about him in the papers, and he seemed anything but lonely or empty. Yet he reacted to her words as if he had been. It made her wonder what he kept hidden from the world.

"Show me the scar," he commanded her, and her feelings of empathy dissolved like smoke.

Tina clenched her teeth together. She wanted to refuse, but what was the point? She *was* pregnant with his child. She'd started this ball rolling down the hill and she had no choice but to go along for the ride.

Angrily, she ripped her shirt from her jeans and shoved the waistband down just enough for him to see the short scar running diagonally across her lower abdomen. She heard his breath hiss in, and then his fingertips slid along her skin, tracing the edges.

Tina went utterly still while inside her body sizzled and sparked like fireworks on New Year's Eve. Flame followed in the wake of his fingers, and pain, as well. Not from the scar—it was too old to hurt—but from the strength of the need that took up residence in her core and refused to abate.

Nico looked up then, his eyes reflecting the same heat that she knew must be in her own. With a strength of will she would have never guessed she possessed, she pushed his hand away and hastily tucked her shirt back in. Her cheeks were hot, and she refused to look at him.

He didn't speak for a long moment. When he did, his voice was more tender than she'd expected it to be.

"It was you."

Tina realized that tears were pricking her eyes. She looked up at him, uncaring if he saw the emotion written on her face.

"I wish it hadn't been," she told him truthfully. Once, she'd fantasized about him, when she'd been young and naive and didn't know what making love meant. She'd wanted him to fall in love with her, to kiss her and marry her and think she was the most beautiful woman alive—that's all she knew when she'd been a teenager, but it had been her happy fantasy for at least a year. And then, once he'd gone away, she'd continued to dream about him.

Yes, she'd wanted him, but not like this. Not with this kind of animosity and mistrust. What had happened between them in Venice, beautiful though it might have been, was a mistake.

His lips thinned, the corners of his mouth white with suppressed anger. Though they were true, she wished she could take back the words, if only to try and rebuild whatever fragile peace they might have made, but it was too late.

The car stopped while she tried to think of something to say, and the driver came to open the door. Silently, Nico ushered her into the obstetrician's office, his fingers firm and burning in her back. His scent wrapped around her senses and made her throat ache with memories of their night together.

The girl on duty at the front desk didn't even look up as they approached. She handed over a clipboard and told Tina to fill it out without ever once making eye contact.

"We are expected," Nico said tightly, "and I am a busy man."

The girl's head snapped up, her eyes widening as she recognized the man standing before her. "Signore Gavretti—I mean, my lord—forgive me. Please come this way."

From that moment on, things moved quickly. Tina was shown into an ultrasound room and made to disrobe. After the technician took images and dated the pregnancy, she dressed and went into the doctor's office where Nico sat silently sending messages on his phone. A few moments later, the doctor arrived and talked to them about her health, the baby and what needed to happen every few weeks.

There would be regular ultrasounds, and at twenty weeks they would know the sex of the baby if they chose. There were vitamins to take, blood tests to have done and urine samples to give.

There were even classes to be taken, though she wasn't sure that Nico would be coaching her through anything when it came to childbirth. And she wasn't sure she wanted him to do so, either.

By the time they left the doctor's office, Tina's head was reeling. Instinctively, she put her hand over her still flat abdomen as if protecting the tiny life growing there.

A baby. She was truly having a baby, and she'd seen the little tiny lump on the screen for herself. Nico had seen it, too, but in the photo the doctor had handed to him in the office. He'd seemed a bit taken aback at first, as if he still couldn't quite believe it, but there was no denying she was pregnant and no denying that the conception date coincided with the night they were together.

Now he was silent as they rode through the streets of Rome. Outside the car window, traffic screeched and honked, but inside it remained eerily quiet.

Eventually, she realized they were not heading in the direction of her hotel. Her heart began to beat a little harder as she turned to him.

"I'm tired, Nico. I want to go back to my hotel and pack." She'd had a text message from Lucia, but she hadn't yet answered it. Since her friend was unable to get together for dinner, it wasn't crucial that she do so right away.

Nico's expression gave nothing away as he looked over at her. He was like a block of ice, so cold and unapproachable that he made her shiver.

"Your suitcases have already been packed." He glanced down at his watch. "I imagine they've been delivered, as well."

An icy tendril of fear coiled around her heart. "Delivered? Where would they be delivered? I'm off to Capri in the morning, and I will need my things tonight."

"I'm afraid the plan has changed, *cara*." His storm cloud eyes were piercing as they caught hers and held them. "We are going to Castello di Casari."

Her pulse beat loudly in her ears. "I can't go with you," she said. "People are expecting me."

"No," he said smoothly, tapping the screen of his phone. "They are not. You are on your own right now, Valentina. Renzo and the lovely Faith are in the

Caribbean and your mother is sailing around Bora-Bora."

Tina stiffened. "While that is certainly true, I do have friends. And they are expecting me." Acquaintances, more like, and they were not expecting her so much as expecting a call from her if she wanted to get together.

Which she typically did not. She was happiest on her own. She'd always been a bit of a loner, and she'd never yet outgrown it. It was part of the reason she liked math and numbers so much. When she was in her head, solving problems, she didn't have to deal with the outside world.

"Then you will call and inform them your plans have changed."

"And for how long should I say I am delayed?" she asked tightly, knowing she was not going anywhere tonight that he did not want her to go.

There was ice in his smile. "Indefinitely."

CHAPTER FOUR

Castello di Casari was far more than an ancient family fortress. It was impenetrable. Nico surveyed the castle rising out of the sheer rock in the middle of Lago di Casari and felt the overwhelming sensation of loneliness and despair that he'd always felt when returning here.

The castle had been modernized over the years, so that its medieval character remained but every modern comfort was provided for. Nico had not been here since his father's death just over a month ago. Why he'd thought to return here now, he wasn't quite certain.

Until he glanced over at the woman sitting stiffly beside him in the helicopter. Yes, it was an excellent place to stash an uncooperative female. He could hardly credit that the woman with the riotous hair and lush mouth was little Valentina D'Angeli, but his brain was becoming more accustomed to the fact by the minute.

Just as it was becoming accustomed to the fact she was pregnant with his child.

Until this afternoon, he would have stated it was impossible, but he'd been thinking back to that night and remembering what he'd done differently with her. He had used a condom, it was true, but he remembered it had torn as he had removed it. Now he wondered if it might have torn earlier and he'd only noticed as the tear grew.

Regardless, she was here and she was pregnant. And he wasn't letting her go, because if he did, he had no illusions that her brother would do everything in his power to keep Nico from the child.

And Nico wasn't allowing that to happen. He kept what was his.

The helicopter sank onto the landing pad and the rotors slowed. A man bent over and approached the craft. Then the door opened and Giuseppe's smiling face was there.

"My lord, we are overjoyed that you have come," the majordomo said.

"It's good to see you again, Giuseppe," Nico replied, descending from the helicopter and turning to assist Valentina.

Giuseppe was a short man, not quite five foot five inches tall, and he tilted his head back to look up at Nico. "I am sorry about your father, my lord. We were all saddened by the marchese's death."

Nico clapped the other man on the shoulder. He didn't feel anything inside, hadn't since he'd gotten the news, but he knew he was expected to show emotion over his father's death. It was the correct thing to do regardless that his father had done nearly everything he could in life to alienate his only son.

"Thank you, Giuseppe. He lived life as he wanted to, *sì?* He died as he lived, and I am sure he is at peace."

Giuseppe's old eyes were suspiciously watery. *"Sì, sì."*

A couple of staff members came forward to collect the luggage as Nico threaded his fingers into Valentina's and brought her to his side. She didn't resist, though he could feel her stiffening as her soft body came into contact with his.

"This is Signorina D'Angeli," Nico said. "She will be staying with us for a while."

Giuseppe didn't betray by word or expression that he understood the significance of Valentina's name, but Nico didn't doubt for a moment that the older man did. Giuseppe followed the motorcycle Grand Prix circuit and would certainly know the famous name. He would never ask questions, however.

"Signorina," he said, bowing over her hand in a courtly gesture. "Welcome to Castello di Casari."

"Thank you," Valentina replied without a trace of the stiffness that Nico could feel in her. He had to admire her ability to appear as if she actually wanted to be here. Giuseppe was none the wiser as she smiled at him graciously.

"We will need a meal in an hour or so," Nico said. "Can you do this, Giuseppe?"

The man dragged his attention back to Nico with some reluctance. *"Sì,* my lord. The chef has been busy since we received the news of your impending arrival."

"Excellent. Please have it served on the terrazzo."

"Sì, my lord."

With another smile at Valentina, Giuseppe went off to oversee the staff. Nico still had her hand captured in his, and he led her across the gray helipad and down the stairs to a door, which was a side entrance to the castle.

"I'm sorry about your father," she said as they entered the modern glass-and-chrome room that his father had built as a waiting room for the helicopter. "I should have said that earlier."

"Thank you," Nico said automatically, though it irritated him to do so. Why couldn't he simply tell the truth? That he wasn't sad? That he felt nothing but anger at the man who'd left him the title and the chaos that went along with it? He was right now pillaging Gavretti Manufacturing in order to repair the damage to all the Gavretti holdings.

He would save his legacy, but at what cost? Now more than ever it was important he do so. He had a child on the way, and he intended to hand over an intact empire when the time came. Unlike his father had done.

"I read that he died of a heart attack," Valentina said from behind him.

"He did." Nico stopped and turned toward her. "He also died with a smile on his face, in the bed of his latest mistress. She was twenty."

Valentina's lips dropped open and he had a sudden urge to close them with his own. To plunder their sweetness for one more glimpse of the bliss he'd felt that night in Venice.

"Oh," she said, her cheeks reddening. Nico wanted to laugh, but he didn't. She was still so innocent, no matter that he'd done his best to corrupt her that night. Desire sliced into him then, hot and sharp.

If anything, it angered him to feel this way toward her. Toward a D'Angeli.

"He had money, *cara,* and a title. Women like that sort of thing, whether they are young or old."

"Not all women," she said.

"This has not been my experience."

She looked haughty. "Then maybe you're not meeting the right kind of women."

"If they are women, then they are the right kind."

She made a noise that sounded like disgust. "How did I ever fall for your smooth words that night?"

He reached out and stroked his fingers along her soft

cheek. She gasped as he did so, but did not pull away. Sparks shot through his skin at the touch, made his body hunger sharply for hers.

Her violet eyes were wide. He wondered if she knew they glittered with heat and need. Whatever this was, she felt it, too. Perhaps, for her, it was the lure of the forbidden. Or perhaps it was simply that he was a man and she a woman and they were attracted to each other.

It didn't have to be complicated, and yet it felt as if it was the most complicated thing on earth.

"You fell," he said softly, "because you wanted to."

She had no signal. Tina tossed her phone onto the bed in disgust. She'd tried several times to send a text to Lucia, but there was no signal out here in the middle of this lake.

This place was, she had to admit, magnificent. She pushed open the double doors onto the balcony, which ran the entire width of the house, and stood in the sunshine. The sun's rays were lengthening as it neared dusk, but her view of the surrounding area was not yet diminished. Castello di Casari sat in the lake, but ringing the lake were mountains punctuated by small villages while vacation homes of the rich and famous perched high on the rocks.

The mountains were deep emerald, blooming with plants and flowers; in the distance, the tallest peaks were wreathed in white. Tina sighed. She could see civilization, but she could not reach it. The castle was built on a small island in the lake, its massive towers and walls taking over the entire island.

She went over to the stone balustrade and leaned against it. Below her, the lake rippled in deep blue currents. There was a sailboat a distance out, and a motorboat zipping by closer in. Pots of pink bougainvillea spilled over in regular intervals around the balcony, and there was a grouping of tables and chairs not too far away. She walked over and sat in one of the chairs, content to sit still and be at peace for a while.

She'd been relieved to find that she had her own room, though she hadn't truly expected Nico would try to share a room with her. What for? He clearly didn't want her anymore, no matter that he strummed his fingers over her skin and her body ached for him.

He had simply done it to prove a point. She had fallen because she'd wanted to, he'd said.

And he was right. She had wanted to. Because she'd been overcome by the feelings and sensations ricocheting through her that night, and because she'd wanted more. She'd wanted to see where the feelings led her.

He, however, had seduced her because she was a woman and she was willing.

Tina snorted in disgust. His father had died in bed with a twenty-year-old. Nico would no doubt do the same someday. What a fine father he would make for her baby. She was beginning to understand why her mother had been so secretive—what if her own father had been so terrible?

Renzo knew who his father was, and it had done nothing but cause him pain. He had not told her that, but their mother had. Renzo's pain was the reason her mother gave for not telling Tina what she wanted to know.

Maybe she'd been right after all.

She sat in the sun until it disappeared behind the mountain. It was still light out, but growing darker much faster now. She still wore jeans and sandals, but she'd removed her jacket and scarf. Now she returned to her room and retrieved them.

There was a knock on her door. The man who had greeted them at the landing pad was there, smiling at her pleasantly. "*Signorina,* his lordship asked me to tell you that dinner is prepared. You can reach the terrazzo by going out on the balcony and taking the steps down to the next level."

"Thank you," Tina replied. She wanted to refuse to join Nico, but she was surprisingly hungry. The anti-nausea medication the doctor had given her had worked wonders and she actually had an appetite for once.

She didn't change for dinner, determined that she would not do that at least. She was here under pro-test, not as a willing guest, so to hell with the niceties. Frau Decker would be horrified at her lack of manners, but Frau Decker was in Switzerland. Besides, her old teacher had never addressed a situation in which a lady might be held captive by a gentleman against her will.

Tina frowned wryly. Whatever would the good woman say if she could see this place and the man who waited at the dinner table? Quite probably, like most women, she would giggle and fawn over him.

Tina went onto the balcony and walked the length of it before finding the stairs down to the next level. There, a large table and at least ten chairs had pride of place beside a stunning view of soaring cliffs directly across the lake.

The table was set for two, with crisp white napkins, crystal goblets, silver flatware and pristine white plates. Nico stood with his back to her, looking out at the cliffs and holding a glass of wine from which he occasion-ally took a sip.

She studied his broad back, reluctant to interrupt

his thoughts and turn them toward her once more. He'd changed, she noted with surprise. Instead of the suit, he wore a pair of stonewashed jeans and a black shirt. His hair curled over his collar, and for a moment she longed to go over and slide her fingers into the silkiness of it as she had done that night.

Tina shivered involuntarily, but not from cold. Her body was hot, her blood thick and syrupy in her veins. He did that to her, and it disconcerted her that he still could.

She took the rest of the steps down and Nico turned, his gaze skimming her lightly as he did so. She tilted her chin up, as she'd been taught, and bore his scrutiny as if it were nothing.

"How are you feeling?" he asked.

"I've been better," she replied.

He appeared concerned. "Do you still feel nauseous?"

Guilt pricked her. "I'm not ill anymore, thanks to the medication. No, I was thinking more along the lines of how this is my first abduction."

She didn't expect him to smile, but he did, and it caught at her heart though it should not. "Mine, too."

"How fortunate," she said crisply. "We can enjoy the experience together."

He came over and pulled her chair out, and she realized she'd actually been standing there as if she'd expected it. How silly, and how very like her at the same time. She only hoped he didn't notice how she blushed.

His fingers skimmed over her shoulders after he pushed her chair in, and twined in her hair. She went very still, sparks zipping along her spine and behind her ears. It hurt, and it felt like the most wonderful thing all at once.

She wanted him to keep touching her, to slide his fingers against her scalp and then along her neck, down to her breasts. She wanted it far more than she should.

And then his breath was in her ear, and a deep shiver rolled through her.

"I would not say *enjoy* so much as endure, perhaps," he said before dropping his hand and taking his own seat.

Tina picked up her water and took a sip. She felt raw inside, exposed, as if he'd seen to the deepest heart of her and knew that her body betrayed her every time he was near. "I was being sarcastic."

His eyes glittered darkly. "Yes, I realize this. And I was simply saying what you were thinking."

They were silent while the food arrived. There was an antipasti platter, a delicate angel-hair pasta in sauce, broiled fish, *verdure* and an array of cheeses. The women who'd brought the meal disappeared and Nico proceeded to serve her. She didn't say anything while he filled her plate. Once he finished, he poured more sparkling water into her glass.

She waited while he began to fill his own plate, but he stopped and looked at her. "Eat, Valentina."

"I will," she said softly. "I'm waiting for you."

"Don't wait."

"It's not polite to start eating."

"To hell with polite. Eat."

She picked up an olive and popped it into her mouth. "Everyone calls me Tina," she said. "You might as well, too."

"If you prefer it."

She shrugged. "I don't, but it's what my friends call me."

He arched an eyebrow, and she couldn't help but

think he looked like the devil, all sinful and dark and tempting. "Are we friends then?"

"Hardly. But Valentina makes me think I'm in trouble." She ate another olive and sighed. "Which I suppose I am, really."

"Are you?"

"It certainly seems that way. I started the day in Rome and I'd made plans to go to Capri. This is not Capri."

He inclined his head. "No, it's prettier. And more exclusive."

She took a bite of pasta. It was delicious and she nearly moaned with the pleasure of eating solid food again for the first time in days. A light breeze blew over them then, and she was glad she'd put her jacket on again. It wasn't unpleasant, far from it, but it would be too cool without sleeves. "Did you grow up here?"

"No."

"I imagine your family has a lot of homes."

"Yes."

Tina pushed an olive around her plate. "Which was your favorite?"

His gaze speared into her then, intense and dark and forbidding. His smooth jaw was tight, and she realized that she'd stumbled into something he didn't want to discuss. It made no sense to her. He'd grown up with so much, while she and Mama and Renzo had lived in tiny apartments in back alleys for most of her childhood.

"I have no favorite," he said shortly. "I spent much of my time away at school."

Sympathy flooded her, though she couldn't imagine his experience being bad. He was an aristocrat, wealthy and very beautiful. He would have been the sun around which the other kids orbited.

"I did, too, once I hit fifteen," she said. "It wasn't a good time to go away."

"It never is." He took a sip of wine. "I went to school when I was six. I came home on breaks until I was seventeen." He shrugged. "So I have no particularly favorite house. I spent more time at school than I did here, or in any of the Gavretti estates."

"I didn't know," she said softly. "I'm sorry."

His eyes were as hard as diamonds. "There is nothing to be sorry about. I received a spectacular education and went to a top university."

"And spent summers with Renzo in the garage," she added.

"Yes."

Tina let out a heavy sigh. "Did you at least enjoy the time you spent with us? I had thought you did, but I was young. It's just that you seemed…happy."

She thought she might have said too much, but he only looked toward the cliffs and didn't say anything for a long moment. "I was," he finally said. "I enjoyed building the prototype with Renzo."

"And yet you left. And Renzo refuses to speak of you to this day. What happened?"

His head whipped around again, his eyes spearing into her. "It's not important."

Impulsively, she reached for his hand, grasped it in hers. His skin was warm, and the blood rushed through her veins just from this contact, making her feel lightheaded and confused.

"It *is* important, Nico. I want you and Renzo to be friends again. I want it to be the way it was."

She thought he would jerk away, but he turned her hand in his, traced his fingers in her palm while she shivered deep inside. "It can never be the way it was, *cara.* You are a woman now, not a child. You know life does not move backward."

Hot tears pressed against her eyelids. "I wish it did. For the sake of our baby, I wish I could fix whatever is wrong between you and Renzo."

Because, no matter what happened between them, he was a part of her life now. Through this baby, the Gavrettis and D'Angelis would always be connected. And it made her sad to think it would not be easy for any of them.

He sat back and let her go. The air wafting over her skin made her feel cold suddenly. "You cannot fix it, Tina. No one can."

She sucked in a deep breath. "I refuse to believe that."

"Then you are a fool."

She looked at him for a long moment. "I refuse to believe that, too," she said, her throat aching.

"Believe what you like, but it does not alter reality," he told her coolly. "Now eat, or we will never leave this table."

She did as he commanded, but only for the baby's sake. The food, which was delicious, failed to give her any pleasure. The more she thought of Nico and her brother, of the way they used to be and the way they were now, the less she tasted of the food.

There had to be a way to repair whatever had gone wrong, if only one of them would tell her about it. She thought of Renzo in the Caribbean with his wife and was thankful they were away for now. She shuddered to think what would happen if he were at home.

It would be a true clash of the titans the next time these men met, and she could not bear the idea she would be the catalyst.

Tina dropped the fork. "I want to know what happens next," she demanded, her heart hot with feeling. He'd taken her from Rome, brought her here, but for what purpose? He couldn't really intend for her to stay with him indefinitely.

Nico glanced over at her, seemingly impervious to the turmoil raging within her. "Dessert, I imagine."

"You know that's not what I mean."

The look he gave her was long and heavy with meaning. Her pulse snapped in her veins until she was certain he must see it thrumming in her neck. Dread lay thick inside her the longer he watched her without speaking.

"Tell me," she said when the silence was more than she could bear. "I have a right to know."

"What do you think will happen, Tina?"

She darted her tongue over her lower lip. "I'm not quite sure. I doubt you intend to keep me here for the next few months, no matter what you implied earlier. That would be ridiculous. And unnecessary."

"I disagree," he said, his voice as smooth as fine wine. "It is very necessary."

"Why?" she asked, apprehension twisting her belly into knots. "I want you to be a part of the baby's life. I won't deny you access."

One dark eyebrow arched. "You say that now. But what about when Renzo returns?" He shook his head. "No, that is not acceptable. You aren't going anywhere, Tina. You're staying here with me."

Tina gripped the edges of her seat and willed herself to be calm. "You can't force me to stay," she said, her voice brittle to her own ears.

He leaned back and spread his hands to encompass their surroundings. "Can I not? We are on an island.

The only way on or off is by helicopter or boat—and I control both of those things."

Her stomach plummeted through the stone floor of the terrazzo even as a chill shuddered through her. "You're being purposely contrary. Renzo will come looking for me. You can't prevent that."

Nico took a leisurely sip of wine, studying her through lowered lids. She endured the scrutiny, though he reminded her once more of a cat singling out prey. She sat very still, waiting for him to spring, knowing she was caught even before he did so.

All she could do was wait and see what manner the attack took.

"No," he finally said, "I can't stop Renzo from looking for you. But even he cannot separate a man and his wife."

CHAPTER FIVE

Tɪɴᴀ's breath was a solid ball in her chest. It sat heavy and thick and she couldn't force it in or out for a long moment.

"You look surprised," Nico said mildly.

Surprised? It was too mild a word for what she was feeling right now.

"I can't marry you, Nico," she choked out.

"Why? Because your brother won't approve?" He made a sound of disgust. "He won't approve of you being pregnant, either. If you cared about his approval, you would not have slept with a strange man that night."

It was too close to the truth, but it angered her nevertheless. "I suppose I deserve that, but it doesn't change the fact that you don't love me. I won't marry a man who doesn't love me."

She didn't know quite where that had come from, but the moment she said it, she knew it was what she felt.

His eyes glittered in the candlelight flickering brighter now that dusk was deepening. "Then you should have thought of that before you spread your legs for me."

Tina gasped, stung by his cruel words. "That's not fair. Women are allowed to take lovers without wanting to marry or have babies with the men they choose."

"Yes, but they are typically more prepared than you were that night."

Her cheeks were aflame. "Oh, yes, it's all *my* fault, right? But I'm not the one who used a faulty condom."

"And I'm not the one who chose a random stranger for my first sexual experience. You were lucky you got me, and not someone who might have treated you with less delicacy than the situation required."

"Well, bravo to you then," she snapped. "But I'm still not marrying you. There is no reason for it."

"I can think of a few reasons, not the least of which is that I'm not giving you—or your brother—a chance to change your mind about letting me be a part of the child's life."

She bowed her head demurely, though her heart was racing a million miles a minute. "I understand why you'd think that, but we can have papers drawn up. I'll sign anything reasonable. We'll make sure everything is spelled out."

He threw his head back and laughed, and a feeling of foreboding ricocheted through her. "How perfectly civil of you, *cara*. But this is not a negotiation. I don't trust you or Renzo. There's nothing you can say, nothing you can promise, that I will believe."

"I give you my word," she said.

"Your word means nothing to me." He shook his head, leaned toward her and trapped her hand in his. "No, you *will* marry me, and just as soon as possible."

Tina thrust her chin out defiantly, though her heart hammered and her insides churned. "Even you cannot compel a woman to marry you because you decree it," she said sharply. "I won't do it."

His eyes narrowed. "How selfish you are, *cara*. You would deprive this child of my name? Of my status? You would allow him to grow up without a legal right to my legacy? Do you think he will thank you for it someday?"

Her heartbeat slowed as his words twisted in her brain. God, she hadn't thought of that. She'd grown up with her mother's name, just as Renzo had, and they'd been just fine in the end—though it hadn't always been easy. There'd been no estate to inherit, no vast sums of money to distribute among heirs. There'd been nothing at all, until Renzo made his fortune.

"It's not about money," she said with certainty. "I have money, and our child will want for nothing."

Not only did she have the money from her trust fund, but she'd also been investing a chunk of it over the years. She now had quite a handsome sum that was all from her own hard work. Her brother might not let her work for him, but she did work—managing her money—and she did a damn good job at it, too.

"I went to boarding school, Tina. I know what it was like. Those girls would have made your life hell, and a big part of that would have been your lack of pedigree. Do you want that to happen to your child?"

Fury vibrated through her then. "I won't send my baby away to school, you can be sure of that."

"It's not only school, though, is it? If you want this child to have every advantage, to have doors open for him and to be accepted everywhere, then you will see that marrying me is the only way to achieve that."

She wanted to press her hands to her ears. "You make it sound so medieval, and yet this is the twenty-first century."

"People are not so changed, though, are they? Especially not in my circles." He leaned forward and trapped her hand where it lay on the table. She tried to pull away, but his grip was as solid as the stone cliffs in the distance. "But there is another, even more pressing reason, darling Tina. If you do not agree to this marriage, I will destroy D'Angeli Motors."

A layer of ice coated her heart. Fear pumped into her in waves. "You cannot," she said, proud that her voice did not break. "If you could, you would have already done so."

He let her go and sat back. "You forget, *cara mia*, that I am a much richer man than I was only a few weeks ago. And I will use that wealth—and the power that comes with this title—to destroy your precious brother if you do not agree to marriage."

Horror seeped into her then. She thought of Renzo, of Faith and baby Domenico, and a wave of guilt swept her. Renzo was happier than she'd ever known him to be now that he'd found Faith. He laughed a lot more these days, and he no longer risked his life on the track. His leg was also on the mend now that the surgeons had removed the scar tissue that had built up over time, and he would very likely be walking without a cane once it healed.

He had everything. How could she put his happiness at risk, especially when she'd created this mess by indulging in a single impulsive act solely for her own pleasure? Renzo had done everything to make sure she had a good life, and this was how she repaid his generosity?

"You are really very cruel, aren't you?" Tina asked, her heart throbbing with fury and hurt.

Nico's expression didn't change, though she thought the corners of his mouth tightened. "Life is cruel," he said. "I am merely doing what I must to protect my child."

"*Our* child."

"Yes, our child." He said the words plainly enough,

and yet there was an inflection there, an unspoken threat. *Our child if you do as I say.*

Tina shivered. It did not go unnoticed.

"Are you cold?"

"A little," she said, unwilling to admit that her shiver was born more out of apprehension than the breeze.

"Then let us go inside."

He came and held out a hand to her. She didn't accept it, pushing herself to her feet without his help. He didn't move away, however, and she found herself trying to take a step backward.

The chair stopped her. He was so close. *Too* close. She could feel his heat crawling into her, surrounding her. His scent filled her senses, spice and man mingled with the aromas of leather and wood.

Heat blossomed in her belly, flowed like a river of syrup into her limbs. She felt as if she'd been drinking when she had in fact not had a drop. He did that to her, had done from the first moment she'd met him on the docks outside the palazzo in Venice.

No, he'd always made her feel funny, though when she'd been younger it had only been a hot, hollow feeling right beneath her breastbone. She'd crept into the garage to feel it, to gaze upon him and daydream.

How deluded she'd been about him. How very, very naive. He was not her dream man, not the husband or lover she could have wished for. He was arrogant, cold and very determined to get his way, no matter the consequences to anyone else.

She despised him. And her body wasn't getting the message. Her body was zinging with sparks, melting, aching. Wanting.

Tina sucked in a sharp breath, reminding herself why she couldn't allow that to happen.

She could never allow it to happen again. He'd consumed her the last time, and she'd willingly let it happen. She'd only panicked when she'd known who he was, not because of what had transpired between them. No, she'd been half-ready to do it again, but she'd let her curiosity get the best of her.

If only she'd never removed his mask!

Tina's first instinct was to drop her gaze from the intensity of his, but she forced herself to look him in the eye. Unflinchingly.

His gaze sparked. Heat spread through her body.

"I won't marry a man who threatens my family," she said firmly.

One eyebrow arched. She had the impression he was mocking her. "Oh, yes? Originally, you said you wouldn't marry a man who didn't love you. Which is it, Tina? Love or duty?"

Tina stiffened. "I won't be compelled against my will."

His expression was doubtful. His gaze dipped, lingered on the scoop neck of her tank top before drifting back up to meet her eyes. "I think you shall, *cara*. If you value the things you claim to."

"You are very certain of yourself," she said, her breath hitching in her throat.

"Indeed."

"Renzo is not an easy mark, and you know it." It made her feel confident to say so, but the truth was she had no idea.

Nico's smile was lethally smug. "Do I? And what if I don't care, *bella mia?* What if I am willing to do anything it takes to win?"

"Even immolate yourself in the process?"

He looked thoughtful for a brief moment. "Perhaps. Are you willing to risk it?"

"Are you?"

He laughed at her. "*Allora*, we shall get nowhere if we talk in circles. Come."

He put his hand on her back then and ushered her inside, through hallways and rooms she hadn't seen earlier. The castle had been modernized, but the rooms were still magnificent. Huge vaulted ceilings soared above her head, painted with frescoes that gleamed with bright blues, deep greens, vibrant reds and creamy flesh tones. The floors were inlaid marble mosaic, punctuated with intricate patterns of lapis and gold, porphyry and malachite.

The old wooden panels lining the walls gleamed with oil and care, and lush sheets of silk damask hung over the floor-to-ceiling windows that she knew would look out on the cool blue beauty of the lake when it was daylight.

She didn't realize he was leading her to her room until he stopped in front of her door. Tina dropped her gaze from his, cursing the timid side of her nature for kicking in when she wanted to face him down like a lioness protecting her brood. Her heart kicked up again at his proximity, at the intimacy of standing in front of her bedroom door with the only man she'd ever shared a bed with.

"Defy me if you wish, but you will realize there is only one choice in the end. You will do the right thing for Renzo and his lovely Faith."

"One choice is not a choice," she replied, her jaw aching with the effort it took not to scream at him.

He shrugged, arrogant and unfeeling to the last. "You can choose what is right, or you can choose to let me compel you into it. Either way, you *will* do what I wish in the end."

"How very generous of you," she said, her voice dripping with sarcasm. "I wonder that you even pretend this is a choice."

He laughed, startling her with the rich sound in the dark and quiet hallway. "You amuse me, *cara*—defiant to the last. I can hardly reconcile this with the girl who couldn't speak to me without turning red."

"I was a child then. I've grown up now."

His gaze slipped over her. "You have indeed. Quite delightfully, I might add." Before she knew what he was planning, his long fingers came up and gripped her chin, holding her head up high for his inspection. "There is a connecting door between our suites. Should you desire a repeat of Venice, you have only to open the door and come inside."

Her heart throbbed in her ears, her neck. Surely he could see her pulse beating. Tina swallowed hard. "I don't," she said. "Never again."

She could see his teeth flash white in the dim hallway. His handsome face was so close, the hard angles touchable. Kissable. *No.*

"Never say never, sweetheart," he told her. "You will lose if you do."

"I hardly think so," she said haughtily.

His head dipped swiftly, and she closed her eyes in reaction. She could feel his breath on her lips, and she shivered with anticipation even while her brain struggled to catch up.

"I think you lie to yourself," Nico said, and then he laughed softly as he pulled away.

Tina's eyes snapped open as her brain finally engaged. She took a step backward, thudded into her still closed door. She'd thought he was going to kiss her. And she'd wanted it.

Fire burned her from the inside out—but was it the fire of shame, or of desire? "I don't want you," she said firmly. "I *don't.*"

His smile mocked her. "Tell yourself that if it makes you feel better. But we both know it's a lie."

Nico sat in the dark with his laptop and went over the figures again. Then he sprawled back in his chair, raking a hand through his hair in frustration.

Even in death, Alessio Gavretti had the power to irritate him. More than irritate him, apparently.

Nico swore softly. He'd spent years trying to impress the man who wasn't impressed with anything—unless it wore a very short skirt and had very large breasts—but his father had always treated him with a cool indifference that had been the hallmark of his personality.

Nothing Nico ever did made a dent in his father's reserve, though the man *had* come to his races a few times. Nico had been the impetus behind Gavretti Manufacturing in the first place, though it hadn't been his original plan when he'd first gone to his father to ask for support. No, he'd wanted to back Renzo—but his father wouldn't hear of it.

"Why should I invest in this man's business when you are perfectly capable of starting your own business, Niccolo? No, build the motorcycles yourself, but do not ask me for money for another."

Nico frowned. That had been a pivotal moment in his life, though he'd not realized it at the time. He'd built the motorcycles, when he'd realized he had no other choice, and he'd lost the only friend he'd ever truly had. It still hurt in places he didn't like to examine, and for that he blamed the woman in his guest room. Without her, he wouldn't be thinking about this so much tonight.

He'd spent so many years not having a conscience that to be reminded it had not always been the case was more unsettling than he would have liked.

He shoved himself upright and went through the open door onto the balcony. It was quiet outside, dark. He welcomed the solitude. The scents of bougainvillea and lavender filled the air, and far below him the waters of the lake lapped at the rock upon which the castle stood.

It was peaceful. And it made him desperate, as well. He could lose it all if he didn't figure this out.

He'd had no idea, until his father had died and the estate had fallen into his hands, just how much of a tangle it was in. Alessio Gavretti had spent money like he had a printing press in the basement—and so had Nico's mother.

They'd separated years ago, but never divorced. His father spent money on women, and his mother spent it on clothing, jewels and homes. Over the years, they'd managed to rack up an impressive roster of loans and long-term debts. It was as if each one had been trying to outdo the other.

Now Nico had to somehow manage to keep the world from knowing how close the Gavretti fortunes teetered to the brink.

He wanted to laugh at the irony. He'd threatened Tina with ruin for her brother if she did not agree to marry him, and yet he was the one who could be ruined if knowledge of the estate's financial matters became public at the wrong moment. He did not doubt that Renzo D'Angeli would snap up Gavretti Manufacturing and sell it off for scrap.

Nico didn't blame him. In his position, he'd do the same—and without a shred of remorse, either.

Nico leaned on the balustrade and peered at the lights of the village in the distance. He couldn't let it happen, and he damn sure couldn't let Tina refuse to marry him. Without a marriage, he would have no claim to his child, especially if she refused to publicly acknowledge him as the father, no matter what she said about papers and signatures.

And why did that matter so much?

It wasn't as if he knew the first thing about being a father, or even that he had latent fatherly instincts coming to the fore. Nor had he wanted a wife or a child to interfere with the way he ran his life. He was free, unencumbered by entanglements, and uninterested in changing the way he lived.

Yes, if he were to let her walk away, he could work on saving the Gavretti estate and think about finding a proper wife later.

Nico snorted. What was a proper wife? His mother had been a proper wife, hand-selected by his father's family, and look how that had worked out. Two bitter, selfish people who'd produced one child and then used that child in their feud against each other.

Anger ate at him, burning in his gut the way it always did when he thought of his parents and the empty childhood he'd had. Oh, he'd had everything money could buy, but he'd lacked the one thing it couldn't: love.

Maybe that was why he'd been so drawn to the D'Angelis. There had only been the three of them, but they'd had enough love in their home to fill him with its glow simply by association.

He glanced over at the glass doors that led from Tina's room. They were shut, the curtains drawn, but there was a light on inside. The light of the television flickered in the gap where the curtains hadn't quite come together all the way.

A wave of longing filled him, stunning him with its potency. He wanted to walk inside there and take her in his arms again, fill her body with his and shut out the world. It was melancholy and stress getting the best of him, he knew that, but it made the feeling no less powerful.

If he were still in Rome, he'd head out to a club for a few hours, call one of the women on his contact list. He'd engage in a night of wanton sex and wake up refreshed and ready to tackle his problems again.

Love had nothing to do with it.

No matter how much he might have longed for his parents' love, or how much he'd admired the D'Angelis' wealth of it, he knew that love was ephemeral in his world. He'd grown up in a family who loved themselves more than each other, and he expected that was how his life would continue. He was thirty years old and he'd never felt even a glimmering of love for another person.

Until the moment Valentina D'Angeli had walked back into his life and told him she was expecting his child. He didn't kid himself that he'd fallen into instant and overwhelming love with this baby, this collection of cells growing in her body, but something *had* happened.

He'd felt as if she'd punched him in the gut, and the feeling hadn't abated over the past few hours. He didn't know what it was, but he wasn't letting her walk away. He hadn't intended to marry her, but in the end he'd realized it was the only way.

Aside from ensuring him access to his child, marrying Tina would give her brother pause. If Renzo did get wind of Nico's financial troubles, he would think twice about ruining the man his sister had married.

Mercenary, yes. But Nico damn well didn't care. He'd been mercenary for so long now that he couldn't bother growing a conscience for one woman. No matter how she tugged at long forgotten memories of acceptance and hope.

CHAPTER SIX

It was midmorning when Tina awoke, and for a moment she couldn't remember where she was. But then it all came back with brutal clarity and she sat up with a gasp. She was marooned in the middle of a lake, held captive by a dark and dangerous man who insisted that she marry him.

She reached for her phone on the bedside table, searching hopefully for a signal, but there was none. Tina tossed the phone down on the plush comforter and made a noise of displeasure.

But what would she do if there were a signal? She'd text Lucia, of course, but she most definitely would not call her mother or Renzo. A shiver slid along her spine at the thought. That would be a disaster.

She flipped the covers back and went to open the heavy silk drapes. The sun filtered in through the laurels, dappling her face with warmth. The lake was alive with windsurfers in the distance, and here and there motorboats zipped by, some towing skiers and others simply out for a leisurely ride.

It was without doubt a gorgeous view and she stared at the green mountains in the distance before turning her attention to getting dressed. Tina showered—and then, just to prove a point, she blow-dried her hair with a round brush until it was stick straight.

When her hair hung smooth and long halfway down her back, she went into the walk-in closet where a staff member had put away all her clothing. Everything was crisp and ready to be worn, so she chose a pair of shantung silk trousers in bright red and a long silk vest in black that belted at the waist. She added a pair of strappy stilettos, just to add a bit of wow factor, and then put on the bangle bracelet her mother had given her for her graduation. She added the rest of her jewelry for the day—diamond earrings, a gold necklace, three rings—before she was satisfied.

No one seemed to be stirring in the house until she reached the kitchen and found the chef and a trio of helpers at work on something that smelled delicious.

"If you will join the *signore* on the terrazzo, *signorina*, breakfast will soon be served."

Tina thanked the woman and went out to the same table she'd shared with Nico last night. He was on the phone, a laptop in front of him, and she stopped to watch the way the sunlight slanted over his perfect features. He seemed oblivious to her presence.

"It stops now," he grated. "You have an allowance. If you burn through it, you will get nothing more until the next quarter."

A second later he smacked his palm on the table, swearing violently. Tina jumped at the sudden movement and spun to go back inside. Before she could reach the door, he called out to her. She turned slowly. He still had the phone to his ear, but he beckoned her over.

Warily, she approached and took a seat while he continued to argue with whoever was on the other end.

Then he ended the call abruptly and slid the ringer to Silent.

"How is it you get a signal out here and I get nothing?" she asked.

"It's the carrier," he told her. "I use a different service when I am here than I do elsewhere. Though sometimes, when the weather is right and you are in the right part of the castle, other signals will come through."

Well, that explained that. "I don't suppose you'd let me use your phone today."

He shrugged. "Why not? You are an intelligent woman, Tina. You won't call your brother and beg him to rescue you."

Her heart thumped. "How can you be so sure?"

He studied her for a moment, his eyes straying over her hair. Warmth blossomed inside her belly then, spreading through her limbs like hot honey. "So it does straighten out," he said thoughtfully.

"I told you so."

"Women have such tricks at their disposal. I would have never guessed."

She almost laughed. "I wouldn't expect you to be au courant about the things that occur in beauty salons. And I did ask you a question, by the way."

He picked up his espresso, his long fingers dwarfing the small cup. "I am aware of it."

"And what is your answer?"

"I already gave you my answer, Tina. You are intelligent and thoughtful. You also love your brother very much. You do not wish to worry him or cause him to cut his vacation short when he is so happy with his new wife and child."

Her pulse throbbed with every word. It was as if he could see inside her soul. She shook herself. That was silly. Of course he couldn't. But he was a very good guesser.

"Besides," he continued, "you are not in danger. You are in a situation of your own making and you refuse to cry wolf before you've thought it all out."

"Not entirely of my own making," she murmured. "It does seem to take two to make a baby."

"Yes, but I've already thought about it and I know what must be done."

"And what if I disagree? I might think myself justified to call Renzo then. He could at least get his best attorneys onto the situation."

His expression remained unconcerned. "By all means, if you think this is the correct course of action. We can fight about who is more suited to get full custody of the child in the courts."

A chill dripped like acid into her veins. She didn't really think he could take her child away from her—but what if he could?

"I haven't made up my mind yet," she said breezily, turning to smile at the woman who brought her a cup of coffee.

"You will," he said with that arrogant assurance that made her want to grind her teeth in frustration.

His phone buzzed on the table and he pressed the button to send it to voice mail without once looking at the screen. She wondered who was on the other end of the line, then realized with an unpleasant jolt that it must be a woman. He wouldn't treat a business associate that way, she was pretty certain, so it had to be a romantic entanglement.

Something twisted in her gut then, some feeling she didn't want to examine too closely. She'd not thought of what his romantic life must be like right now. They'd spent a single night together nearly two months ago. Though he'd not been linked with any particular woman in the papers lately did not mean there wasn't one—or had not been one that night.

A wave of queasiness swept through her, but it had nothing to do with pregnancy hormones. She pushed the coffee away.

"You can drink it," Nico said. "It's decaf."

For some reason, she was ridiculously touched that he'd known she couldn't have caffeine. But she shouldn't be. It wasn't a romantic gesture; it was a practical one. "Thank you for remembering."

The smile he gave her threatened to melt all her good intentions to remain detached and controlled. How could she even begin to feel that way? He was threatening her—threatening her family. But what he said next cracked the ice she tried to keep around her heart.

"I spent a couple of hours this morning looking up pregnancy. I admit I know nothing."

Tina swallowed. Hard. "I'm afraid I don't, either. I had thought to beg Faith for information."

Nico looked suddenly thoughtful, and the ice cracked a little more. "There is a website with pregnant women on it. They talk about everything. You can even track the stages of your pregnancy. It is quite amazing."

Tina picked up her cup with shaky fingers—mostly because she needed something to do—and took a sip.

She didn't want to see this side of him, not when he'd threatened her with a custody battle and harm to her family if she didn't bow to his will. But when he looked at her like this, when he spoke so earnestly and honestly it made her heart hurt, she remembered the old Nico, the one who used to work in the garage with Renzo and laugh freely.

And remembering made her ache with longing to see them reconciled, though he'd told her yesterday that would never happen. How could it be that bad between them? That unforgivable?

"I'll look into it," she said softly, keeping her eyes downcast while she worked to find her center.

The food arrived then, and once more they were alone and eating together on this gorgeous balcony overlooking the beautiful azure lake. Everything was delicious and plentiful, and she found herself eating more than she'd thought she would be able to.

"I'm glad to see you eat," he said. "You were very pale yesterday when I first saw you."

"The medication helps tremendously. I'm just happy I didn't miss breakfast. I thought I'd slept too late."

His eyes gleamed like purest silver in the shaft of sunlight slanting through the laurels. "You will never miss breakfast so long as you are here, *cara*. The meal will wait until you are ready for it."

A dart of pain pierced her right in the center of her chest and she found herself blinking rapidly to dispel the tears that threatened to fall. Why? *Why?*

It was nothing to cry over. It was ridiculous to think of crying. Niccolo Gavretti was not holding meals for *her*. He was taking care of her because she carried his child, nothing more.

She absolutely would not read more into the gesture than it contained. He was *not* being thoughtful.

But when had anyone ever put her needs and feelings first? When had anyone ever treated her as if she were the center of *their* universe?

Mama and Renzo loved her, she had no doubt, but Renzo had always been the one around whom the family orbited. Because he was male. Because he was older.

Because he was wildly, insanely driven and successful. She'd grown up in his shadow. It hadn't been a bad place to be, but it had also not been a place where she could flourish on her own merits.

"Thank you," she managed to say finally. "That's very kind of you, but there's no need to hold meals for me. Tell me what time you wish to have breakfast, and I will be here for it."

His phone buzzed again, startling her. Again, he sent it to voice mail without looking at the screen. He did it so casually that she almost felt sorry for the person on the other end of the line.

"We will eat when you are ready. A pregnant woman needs plenty of sleep."

Heat suffused her then, made her skin glow. There was something about the way he said *pregnant woman* that made her blush. Absurd.

"I will still endeavor to awaken at a reasonable hour," she said stubbornly. "You shouldn't have to wait for me."

He grinned, and her heart squeezed tight. So, so handsome when he wasn't scowling—and even when he was, damn him. "Truthfully, *cara mia,* I am a night owl. I prefer to sleep in myself. But if you begin to awaken at dawn, then dawn is when breakfast will be."

Tina shuddered. "Never fear, dawn is definitely not my style."

He reached for a roll. "Perhaps this night owl lifestyle will do us well when we have a newborn to take care of. I understand they do not sleep much."

Tina could only gape at him. "Exactly how much reading have you been doing anyway?"

Though, truthfully, that wasn't why she was stunned. No, it was the implication that *we* would be taking care of a newborn. Not her. Both of them, as if he, too, would get up in the middle of the night to feed the baby.

It was a mental picture she did not need.

"I couldn't sleep last night, I'm afraid." He picked up his coffee. "Do you have any idea how much work a baby can be?"

"I have some idea," she said, thinking of Renzo and Faith and the haggard, sleepless looks they'd worn for the past few months.

He looked so serious. "It's rather frightening how much attention such a little person needs."

"Well, they can't do it themselves."

"No," he agreed.

His phone buzzed again. This time he glanced at it before swearing and sending it to voice mail. It was just what she needed to pierce the bubble of dazed delight swirling around her head. He would not lull her with talk of babies.

"Why don't you just answer it?" she asked a bit more sharply than she intended.

There was a sudden chill that blanketed his eyes, and she almost wished she'd kept her irritation to herself.

"Because it will do no good," he told her mildly, though she wasn't fooled he was anything other than angry about the calls. "Some women are incapable of listening to reason, and I refuse to bash my head against the wall repeatedly in an effort to be heard."

Tina's spine stiffened. "I'm rather surprised you would even bother. I thought your usual method was simply to leave once you were finished."

His eyes glittered so hotly she had an urge to apologize. But she wouldn't.

He stood and pocketed the phone, and she couldn't

quite shake the feeling she'd insulted him. Though why she should care, she couldn't say.

"Sadly," he said, "there are some women in a man's life that it is impossible to leave. No matter how much he might wish it."

The island was larger than Tina had first thought when they'd arrived yesterday. On the other side of the castle was a terraced garden, with grapevines twining over a pergola, cobbled walkways, and plots of herbs and flowers. There was also a stone pool with clear turquoise water that looked as if it, too, had been carved out of ancient rock and set here during Roman times.

It had been hours since breakfast. She'd spent some time exploring the castle, and when she'd realized there was actually a garden, she'd changed her shoes into something more reasonable so that she could investigate it further.

She skirted the pool and walked across the grass toward the vine-shaded pergola. From the outside, it looked so private and cool. Peaceful. She could use a little bit of peace in her life right now.

She hadn't seen Nico since this morning, but she hadn't stopped thinking about their exchange on the terrace. *There are some women in a man's life that it is impossible to leave. No matter how much he might wish it.*

Like a woman who was pregnant with his child? She felt like a fool the more she thought of it. Of course he didn't want her in his life, but he was willing to accept her because of the baby. If she married him, would she be the woman on the other end of that phone someday?

She ran her hand along a stand of tall ornamental grass, enjoying the way the fuzzy tops tickled her fingers. No doubt she *would* be the woman on the other end of the phone, whether she married him or not. They were having a baby together and they would always need to be in contact with each other, regardless of whether or not they married.

He would be in her life, and she in his, for as long as they lived. The thought made her shiver—only it wasn't completely out of fear or anger that she did so.

No, more like excitement.

Tina stopped in the middle of the garden as her legs seemed to suddenly be made of jelly. My God, a baby was such a game changer. A *life* changer. A child was forever. It was such a huge obligation that Tina sucked in an abrupt, sharp breath, heavy with responsibility and unshed tears.

My God.

What had she gotten herself into? It was too much. *Too much...*

Her heart beat hard. She thought of Faith and Renzo, of the baby they both loved so much. She could see the pride in their gazes, the love and the utter conviction they would do anything it took to protect their child. And each other.

Tina passed beneath the pergola and found an outdoor furniture grouping plush with overstuffed cushions. It was a perfect place to curl up and read—or to think.

She sank onto the couch and lay back against the pillows. Tears pricked her eyes. Such a mess she was in. Nico didn't love her, nor she him, but they'd created this life together. This tiny life that would need so many things from her.

Certainly she could hire a nanny. She could buy her own house and hire around-the-clock care for her child. She could do this alone, she didn't doubt it.

But was it fair to her baby to make him or her shuffle between parents?

Tina put a hand over her belly and concentrated on breathing. Her heart hurt with the chaos of her thoughts. Was agreeing to marry Nico the right thing to do? She pictured Renzo and knew he would be furious if she did.

But if marrying Nico kept him from going after Renzo or D'Angeli Motors, then she had to do it. She would not be responsible for this feud between them growing any worse, nor would she be responsible for bringing harm to her brother and his family.

The sun was warm beneath the pergola, though she was not in direct light. She lay there for a very long time, gazing out at the bright green lawn with red and pink flowerbeds, pencil pines, bay laurels, and even a small grove of olive and lemon trees, until her eyes started to droop.

Tina awoke with a start sometime later, a chill skating over her skin as the sun's warming caress moved on to another part of the garden. Birds chirped in the trees and she could hear the distant sounds of church bells from the nearest village across the lake.

She'd been dreaming about Nico, as he used to be when he came to their house so many years ago. He'd laughed then. Smiled. He'd always had an edge, but it hadn't seemed frightening the way it did now.

Now she was utterly convinced he would do whatever it took to get his way. Ruthlessly.

"You scared Giuseppe out of several years of life when he could not find you," came a cool voice.

Tina gave a little gasp of fright. She turned, found the man she'd been dreaming about sitting in a chair across from her, watching her with an intensity that both warmed and frightened her.

"I'm sorry," she said automatically. "I fell asleep."

"I see that."

She pushed herself upright on the cushions and stretched like a cat coming to life after a long nap. "I don't know what happened. It was warm and cozy, and I couldn't keep my eyes open."

He looked around the sheltered pergola as if seeking the answer somewhere in the leafy green vines. She realized then that they were hidden from the view of anyone in the castle. A person would have to walk across the garden and cross in front of the pergola to see anyone inside it.

No wonder Giuseppe had lost her. She felt a pinprick of guilt as she thought of the little man searching. He'd been nothing but wonderful to her since the moment she'd arrived. He, at least, made her feel like a guest instead of a prisoner.

"It is a lovely spot for a nap," Nico said. "I believe I might have fallen asleep here once when I was six."

Her heart flipped as she thought of him as a little boy. Had he frightened his parents when he'd disappeared that day? Or had they known where he'd gone and left him to sleep in this lovely bower?

He seemed distant, his eyes focusing on some faraway point. Then he swung his gaze back to her. It was cool, hard. Determined. "It is time, Tina."

She swallowed. "Time for what?"

He flicked his fingers against his jeans, as if removing a speck of dirt. "Time to choose."

Her heart skipped. "Who was the woman on the phone?" she asked, fresh anger surging in her veins.

His eyes darkened. She didn't think he would answer. But he surprised her.

"My mother. We were arguing."

Tina ducked her head and studied her clasped hands. So much rage in so few words. She felt as if she'd invaded his privacy somehow, yet she'd had to know the answer. As if it mattered when he compelled her to marry him with threats to her family.

"It's none of my business. I shouldn't have said anything."

She could feel his gaze still on her, intense, steady, penetrating. "You heard me fight with a woman. You saw me ignore her calls. And I've asked you to marry me. You have every right to be curious, under the circumstances."

"Actually," she said, her heart thudding as she lifted her gaze and met those storm-cloud eyes, "you didn't ask me. You told me."

He was so beautiful sitting across from her, his long legs stretched out in front of him, one arm hooked along the back of the big chair as he sprawled casually in it. He wore dark jeans and a white shirt, unbuttoned to show a perfect V of tanned skin that she could remember kissing—innocently at first, reverently later.

He arched an eyebrow as he studied her. She knew her color was high and wondered what he must be thinking. As if it mattered. As if anything but what he demanded of her mattered.

He ran his fingers along the arm of the chair in an absent gesture. "What is the difference? The outcome will be the same."

Her temper flared. "A woman wants to be asked, Nico. It's part of the fantasy."

"Does this mean you've come to your senses?"

Her breath caught, her blood pounding in her temples, her ears. Come to her senses? She felt as though she'd lost them two months ago.

"Promise you won't harm my family or D'Angeli Motors." She said it firmly, her heart racing recklessly fast. It wasn't like her to be so bold, and yet she'd been bolder in the past twenty-four hours with him than she'd ever been in her life. Oh, she was assertive enough usually, having learned to come out of her shell after years of schooling, but not confrontational. She'd been taught to be polite, gracious and ladylike—skills that were somehow lacking when she faced Niccolo Gavretti.

One corner of his mouth turned up. It could not be called a smile. "So long as Renzo leaves me alone, then I will do the same."

Tina closed her eyes, her entire body quivering with fear and anticipation all at once. Was she really going to do this?

Of course she was. What choice did she have? She wouldn't let her family suffer. Nico was titled, wealthy and no doubt in possession of far more power now that he'd inherited his father's estate. Renzo would be no match for him. And she would not let that happen.

"Then you should ask me," she said. "It would be the proper thing to do."

She didn't expect him to do what he did next. He rose from the chair in a graceful movement. And then he was at her side, sinking onto a knee on the gray stone cobbles in front of the couch. His palm came up, cupped her cheek, while his other hand took one of hers and brought it to his heart. It was a grand gesture, even if it was false.

Tina turned her cheek into his palm, though she did not mean to do so. But it was such a tender touch, and she'd ached to feel it for so long. For nearly two months. It stunned her to discover that she'd missed him, missed the aching rightness of his skin against hers.

Oh, she was in so much trouble here.

"Valentina D'Angeli," he said, his fingers suddenly stroking down, along the column of her neck, making her shiver with longing. "Will you be my wife?"

Tina darted her tongue over her lips. She was insane, insane—*insane*—for even considering this. But he was right; she had no choice.

It was the correct thing to do. For her family. For her baby.

"Yes," she whispered, her throat constricting on the word. "Yes."

CHAPTER SEVEN

TINA closed her eyes as his head descended, anticipating his kiss. Longing for it. It had been so long since she'd felt the hot press of his mouth against hers and she was surprised at how much she wanted it. Oh, it was wrong, but she wanted it.

For all her breathless anticipation, however, he did not kiss her. Or, he did kiss her, but not the way she wanted. His lips feathered along her cheek before he tilted her head down and placed a chaste kiss on her forehead.

Disappointment lanced into her as he stood and helped her to her feet.

"There is much to do, *tesoro*," he said. "You will need to pack an overnight bag."

Tina blinked in confusion. "An overnight bag? Why? Are we going somewhere?"

He put his hands on her shoulders, skimmed them down her bare arms. His touch left her glowing and hot, like burning embers on a cool spring night. "We are going to Gibraltar," he told her.

Tina's heart plummeted. "Gibraltar?"

He frowned, but it wasn't unfriendly. "You know why couples go to Gibraltar, Tina. You cannot be that sheltered."

She shook her head as a tide of apprehension began to bubble to life inside her. "I do know why. But why must we? I had thought—"

His pitying look told her he knew exactly what she'd thought. That they would have a normal, though perhaps hurried, wedding. That she would spend the next month or so choosing a gown, flowers, a cake and a venue. That she would somehow persuade Renzo to put aside his dislike and give her away.

She was exactly like other girls in that she'd always imagined she would have a fairy-tale wedding.

But it was not to be. She'd done everything backward, and now this man she barely knew anymore, this man she'd agreed to marry, was taking her to Gibraltar for a quickie wedding. They would be married within twenty-four hours of their arrival on the rock. She would be Signora Gavretti—

But no, she would be the marchesa di Casari.

Tina's knees melted like butter and she nearly sank onto the soft cushions again. Nico steadied her, his strong arms coming around her and pulling her close.

"There is no need to wait," he told her even as he held her against the heat and hardness of his body. "No need to prevaricate."

"But my family..."

His eyes flashed hot. "I am your family now, Tina."

By nightfall, they were on his private jet, winging their way across the Mediterranean toward Gibraltar. Nico sat across from her, his laptop open, his gaze fixed on the screen, while Tina couldn't seem to concentrate on the book she'd been trying to read. Her eReader sat on her lap, forgotten, as she stared at her own sad reflection in the jet's window.

Her life had changed so fast. Two months ago, she'd been looking forward to a masquerade party with Lucia. Everything she'd thought about her life up to that point had been blasted apart in the space of one night, though she had not known how completely it would change her at the time.

Just a little fun, she'd thought. The chance to be someone different, someone more free and spontaneous. Someone brave and bold and in control.

Ha. Some control.

With Niccolo Gavretti, she had no control. She slanted her gaze toward him, her breath catching as it always did when confronted with the evidence of his staggering male beauty. He frowned as he studied the screen, his fingers tapping a key here and there.

She wanted to go to him, wanted to smooth the frown from his face—and she wanted to run away at the same time. She had never been so tormented over one male in her life as she had over this one.

Always this one.

He looked up then and caught her watching him. She didn't jerk her gaze away, didn't try to hide that she'd been looking. What was the point? He closed the laptop and put it away.

"I know this isn't the way you expected this to happen," he said. "But it's for the best."

"The best for whom?" she asked automatically.

His silver gaze didn't waver. "For us. For the baby."

"I don't think waiting a month would have hurt."

He shrugged. "When I decide to do a thing, I do it. I see no point in waiting."

When *he* decided.

"What about your mother? Don't you think she might like to see her son get married?"

His laugh was unexpected. It also sent a shiver over her. "The only thing she cares about right now is the fact I'm forcing her to live on her allowance. I doubt she'd trouble herself to bring me water if I were dying of thirst on her doorstep."

Sadness jolted her at that statement. She knew he was an only child, and of course she knew that his father had recently died, but she'd had no idea his relationship with his mother was that bad. "Perhaps she's still upset over your father's death. Grief does unexpected things to people."

She felt a little foolish for saying such a thing considering how his father had died, but stranger things had happened than a wife still being in love with her philandering husband.

He stared at her disbelievingly. "She is not sad, *tesoro*. Or, if she is sad, it's not because he died, but because I'm now in charge of the money."

"I'm sorry," she said because she didn't know what else to say.

"Not all families enjoy each other's company the way yours does."

Tina dropped her gaze from his. Yes, her family loved one another, there was no doubt about it. But she also thought perhaps they failed to understand one another, as well. They would absolutely not understand, for instance, why she'd agreed to marry Nico.

No, they would be furious. Renzo would pop a gasket when she told him.

Nico's phone rang and he took the call, ending their conversation. A short while later, the plane landed at Gibraltar airport. It was dark when they stepped off the plane. She couldn't see the ocean, but she could smell the tang of the salt air.

They climbed into a waiting car and were whisked to an exclusive hotel high above the city. They checked into the penthouse suite, which the staff assured them came with breathtaking views of the Bay of Gibraltar and the Spanish mainland—as well as the Rif Mountains of Morocco—though it would be morning before they would see the view.

But once they entered the suite, Tina was more concerned about the room. *Room*, as in singular.

"We need another room," she said to Nico when she realized there was only the one.

She wasn't ready to spend the night with him, not like this. Not when everything was spiraling out of control and she felt as if her life was no longer her own. If he'd kissed her earlier beneath the pergola, she might have yielded to him like a flower bending in a storm.

But he had not, and she'd had several hours now to fret about what was happening. From the moment she'd agreed to marry him, he'd shifted into high gear. She should have realized that he would. He was a businessman, and he had every intention of closing the deal before anything could happen to derail his plans.

To him, she was another acquisition. A bit of land, a factory, an exclusive source of some necessary component for his motorcycles.

What did you expect?

Nico crossed the main living area and opened the balcony doors. The bay spread like spilled ink below, and the lights of ships lit up the harbor. Across the bay, the Spanish town of Algeciras glowed in the night.

"There is only this room, *cara*," he said when she came to stand in the open doorway.

Tina crossed her arms over her chest, her heart thrumming along like she'd just had a caffeine injection. "It's happening too fast for me, Nico. I only said yes this afternoon, and now we're here, and we're in the same room together, and my head is spinning."

He turned his head to look at her. She couldn't read him, couldn't tell what was in that enigmatic gaze of his, and her pulse skipped. He was probably annoyed she was giving him trouble.

"There is only one room because it's all they have available, Tina. We'll figure it out, I'm sure."

He sounded cool and guarded, and so very reasonable. Her cheeks felt hot. Sex seemed to be the last thing on his mind, though she couldn't seem to move it from the front of hers. Because she couldn't help but remember the last time they'd been alone in a hotel room overnight.

This one might be sleek and modern, furnished with chrome-and-glass tables, flokati rugs and leather couches, nothing at all like the elegant Hotel Daniele, but her mind didn't know the difference. It kept replaying images of their last night together—cotton sheets so fine they felt like silk, twining bodies, sleek skin and that one perfect moment when she'd discovered how very addictive good sex could be.

"There is a couch," she said, resisting the urge to fan herself.

His expression did not change. "I am aware of it."

She hoped her cheeks weren't as red as they felt. "I'll sleep on it. I'm smaller than you."

He left the railing and stalked toward her. She dropped her arms to her sides, took a step backward. He was so very big, so near, as he stopped only inches away from her. She had to tilt her head back to look up at him, and she wished that she'd put the stilettos back on. At least she wouldn't feel as if he loomed over her if she had.

He reached out and caught a lock of her hair in his hand, twined it gently around his fist. "Is this really what you want?"

She nodded once, quickly.

He lifted her hair to his fine, aristocratic nose. "Do you not think, *cara*, that perhaps the modesty is a bit misplaced?"

The heat threatened to incinerate her from the inside out. "I—I agreed to marry you. So you would not harm my family," she said, her voice little more than a hoarse whisper.

He laughed softly, wrapped her hair once more around his fist until she had to move closer. "Ah, I see. You have given yourself to me as a sacrificial lamb, is that it?"

"No—"

"You think that because you've agreed to the marriage, sex is off the table?" His voice was slightly harder this time.

She swallowed. "I didn't say that. But they are two different things, are they not? We hardly know one another."

"And we knew each other not at all in Venice. I seem to remember this made the entire evening more exciting, not less. Shall I procure a couple of masks to make it easier for you?"

She dropped her chin, hiding her eyes from his. Not because she was embarrassed or ashamed, but because if she did not he would see the flare of excitement that even now dripped into her bloodstream, drugging her with need.

"That was different. And there were consequences neither of us expected."

His playful tone disappeared. "I fail to see how these consequences affect the topic at hand. Or how sex on one night is different than sex on another. Unless, of course, it's the man you object to and not the sex."

That wasn't it at all, and yet she couldn't tell him that. She'd already lost so much of herself to him—if they spent the night together, how much more would she lose?

"I—I'm not ready," she said, still keeping her eyes downcast. "It's not you. It's me."

She felt him go completely still. "How…amusing," he murmured, before he dropped her hair and stepped around her, into the room and away from the currents swirling between them.

Tina's throat was thick with words that would not come, with feelings and emotions she did not fully understand. She'd blundered, and yet she'd only been trying to preserve her sense of self for a little while longer.

He prowled across the carpet, his shoulders tight as he opened the liquor cabinet and poured a finger of Scotch into a glass before turning back to her, the drink cradled in his hand.

"No matter what you might think, *cara*, I am in full control of my libido. You waste your time imagining that I intend to take you to my bed and have my wicked way with you. We have one bed because one bed is all that was available. You may sleep in it unmolested, I assure you."

He downed the Scotch and grabbed his briefcase. "I have work to do, and no inclination to coerce you into doing something which is obviously distasteful to you."

* * *

Tina awoke the next morning in the bed, though she'd started the evening on the couch. She sat up groggily and swung her head toward the direction of the bathroom. The sound of the running shower came through the closed door. A few minutes later it stopped, and then Nico strode into the room wearing nothing but a towel slung low over his hips.

Tina bit off a gasp as she grabbed the sheet and pulled it up to her chin. Nico stopped in his tracks, his expression wry.

"You're wearing the same thing you wore when you went to sleep on the couch, Tina."

She glanced beneath the sheet. So she was, though her attire hadn't quite been the foremost thing on her mind. She let the fabric fall again as hot embarrassment crept through her. He had to be laughing at her on the inside for acting like a startled virgin—though that was not why she'd gasped.

No, she'd gasped because seeing him nearly naked like that was an assault on her senses.

And she wanted more.

"I was fine on the couch," she said, pushing those thoughts away. "You didn't have to bring me in here."

"You didn't look fine. You looked cramped. And cold." He reached into the closet and took out a pair of khaki trousers. Tina jerked her gaze away automatically when he dropped the towel—and then swung it back with a sense of glee. He stood with his back to her so that she could look to her heart's content without him being the wiser. And what a view it was: muscled shoulders, narrow waist, tight buttocks and long, strong legs.

Something flared to life in her belly, something hot and dark and hungry. She gripped the sheet in her fists. Oh, my…

She didn't remember him carrying her into the bedroom last night—and yet she did remember one detail. She remembered shivering and curling up tight under the blanket, and then something warm and solid had cradled her until she forgot she'd been cold.

But had it only been him carrying her, or had he lain down in the bed and held her tight? She didn't know, and she didn't want to ask.

He slid into a pair of briefs before pulling on the khakis and flipping through the closet for a shirt. When he turned back to her, the dark shirt hung open to the waist, affording her a view of sculpted chest and abs that made her mouth water. Tina bit her lip to stifle a whimper.

Nico's gaze was sharp as he looked over and caught her staring at him. "Never fear, *cara*, you slept unmolested. I prefer that my bed partners participate in the activities. It is much more fun that way."

Tina let her gaze drop. "I did not doubt it," she said, because she knew that if he *had* tried to make love to her, she wouldn't have slept through it. "Thank you for making sure I was warm again."

He shrugged as he began to button the shirt. "You are the mother of my child, Tina. Regardless of how this began between us, I will take care of you. Nothing is more important than this baby."

Her stomach hollowed. Of course the baby was the most important thing—and yet it hurt to hear him say it. To him, she was a possession, a vessel carrying a precious cargo. The thought made her ache inside. What would it be like to marry a man who loved her? To have him be excited about the baby instead of resigned?

"I have business to take care of," he told her when he finished dressing. "The wedding will be this evening, so try to amuse yourself for a few hours."

Tina sat in the middle of the big bed once he was gone, feeling dejected. Amuse herself. So typical. He went off to run his company and expected her to entertain herself until he returned.

He was exactly like her brother in that respect—except that Faith had kept working for Renzo until she'd hired her own replacement. There was no way Renzo would dare to tell Faith she couldn't do what she wanted to do.

Even now, Faith oversaw his calendar of appointments and basically ran his entire life while taking care of a newborn. Faith was loved and valued and, though Tina would have never thought it possible with her macho brother, she was very much his equal. His other half.

It was his attitude toward his wife that had given Tina the hope he would eventually cave to her desire to work in the D'Angeli accounting department. She knew he'd been worried she couldn't handle the pressure, the people, or that her innate shyness would somehow stop her from fitting in. He was wrong, though she didn't suppose she would get the chance to show him that now.

Tina showered and breakfasted, then decided to go for a swim in the hotel pool. The exercise would do her good and it would make the time pass until evening. But first she checked her phone for messages.

There was an email from her mother, who was having the time of her life in Bora-Bora, and a quick text from Faith with a picture of baby Domenico and Renzo.

Tina's throat hurt as she swallowed tears. Renzo and Faith were so happy, while she and Nico were merely going through the motions. What would it be like to be so overwhelmingly happy? So in love?

She pushed those thoughts down deep and went

down to the pool. She swam laps for a while, and then sat in the shade of an umbrella and stared at the harbor below. Her thoughts kept going around and around. She almost called Lucia, just to have someone to talk to, but she didn't know what to say. How could you tell anyone that you were pregnant and about to marry the baby's father even though he did not love you?

It was too pitiful, and so she sat and stared at the blue water until she finally gave up and returned to the penthouse suite.

The last thing she expected to find as she opened the door was a seamstress and a selection of wedding dresses. Shock rooted her to the spot as she stood in the entry with the key card in her hand and the door wide-open.

There were racks of gowns—gorgeous, expensive gowns with lace and silk and pearls—that must each have cost a small fortune.

He'd ordered them without her knowledge. Without her input. He'd made the choice for her, just as he'd made so many other choices since barging back into her life in the Pantheon.

It hurt in ways she hadn't imagined possible. She was already feeling sorry for herself, feeling like a burden and a possession rather than a cherished companion and equal after seeing Faith's text earlier, and her hurt feelings bubbled over until she had to act or burst with the effort not to.

She spun on her heel and marched into the office, uncaring that she was still in her bikini and flimsy cover-up.

Nico was not alone. Three men looked up in surprise when she entered the room. Nico's expression could have stopped a bear in its tracks—but she refused to

be intimidated. The two men with him excused themselves, slipping out of the office and leaving them alone.

She stood with her hands on her hips, glaring at him.
It was only when his gaze dropped down her body that
she realized the pose thrust her breasts forward. It was
all she could do not to hug herself, but she refused to
shrink beneath his simmering gaze.

He met her eyes again, a flicker of interest kindling
in his. "What is this about, Tina?"

She took a step toward him, her heart thundering in
her chest. "Wedding dresses? You picked out *wedding
dresses* for me?" She was so angry that she could barely
get the words out without them tripping over each other.

His brows drew down. "No, I did not," he said evenly.
"You may pick what you want. I only asked for several
for you to choose from."

She dropped her hands to her sides, clenching her
fists together rhythmically. Violent emotion swept
through her. He was no different from her brother in
the way he viewed her. No, he *was* different. Renzo
might view her as an accessory, but he loved her. This
man did not.

At least Renzo didn't think so little of her that he
would pick out her clothes for her.

*No, but he picked your schools. And when you
wanted to major in finance, you had to convince him
he should approve.*

She was so damn tired of men making decisions for
her. It was going to stop. Now.

"I don't want any of them," she said tightly. Angry
tears threatened to spill over as she worked to control
her temper. She knew he thought she was being un-
reasonable, but she didn't expect him to understand.
How could he?

He waved his hand as if it were nothing. As if she were a bothersome mosquito flitting around his head. "Then send them away. It's nothing to get upset about."

"You have no idea, do you?" she flung at him. "Women are taught from the time they're little girls to look forward to their wedding day. There are entire magazines dedicated to weddings—to gowns! You don't pick a woman's dress, or pick a selection of dresses, and tell her to choose one. It's arrogant, unfeeling—what are you doing?"

He'd stepped around the desk and started moving toward her, stalking her, until she backed into the closed door with a gasp.

He looked angry—and so very handsome he stole the breath from her lungs. When he reached out and hooked an arm around her, she could only squeak in surprise. Then he hauled her against his hard body until she was pressed to him, breast to belly to hip.

"How is this for unfeeling?" he growled before his mouth came down on hers.

CHAPTER EIGHT

FOR a moment, Tina was stunned into immobility. But only for a moment.

Though her brain told her to resist his kiss, she wound her fists into his shirt instead and arched her body into his. He threaded one hand in her hair and tilted her head back, his other hand sliding down to cup her bottom.

Excitement shot through her in a chain reaction of sparks and sizzle and longing so sharp it made her moan.

She thought that she'd remembered what kissing him was like, but she hadn't remembered even a tenth of it. He consumed her, his tongue sliding against hers, his mouth demanding everything she could give.

Had it been like this in Venice? Yes—and no. Yes, he'd kissed her with this kind of passion—but he hadn't kissed her without restraint. Now there was no restraint. He was a sexual animal, pushed to the edge of control, and she welcomed his fierceness.

His kiss turned her inside out, and she only wanted more.

His hand slid beneath her cover-up—beneath her bikini—and she gasped. He cupped her bare bottom, squeezed, pulling her harder against him until she could feel his erection straining against her abdomen.

Liquid need melted into her core. She wanted him, wanted to feel his body inside hers again. She wanted that perfect storm of passion and heat, the tactile pleasure of touching him everywhere.

She'd never felt more beautiful, more alive and wonderful, than she had when they'd made love the last time. She desperately wanted that feeling again even if it was bad for her. Even if she'd wake up afterward, feeling hungover and hating herself for giving in.

She. Did. Not. Care.

Tina yanked his shirt from his trousers, desperate to feel his bare skin beneath her palms, but a sudden noise outside the door startled her and brought her crashing back to reality.

There were people out there. And dresses. Dresses that had made her so angry she'd come in here to confront him about his lack of respect for what she might want.

But before she could summon the energy to push him away, he stepped back abruptly. He looked wild, his eyes gleaming, his hair mussed where she'd threaded her fingers into it. Not only that, but his body was still aroused, still ready for her. She could see the outline of an impressive erection straining against the fabric of his khakis.

A part of her wanted to close the distance between them, unzip him and wrap her hand around that steely velvet part of him.

But she wouldn't. She wasn't that bold. And besides, she'd come in here for a different reason altogether. A reason she'd forgotten the instant he'd touched her.

"*That* is why we are marrying," he said, his voice

lashing into her with its coolness as he tucked in his shirt again. "Not because this is a fantasy, or a love affair, or any other reason that suits your romantic sensibilities. We are marrying because we have passion, *cara*. And because, as you so helpfully pointed out to me last night, there were consequences to that passion."

He turned and walked back to his desk, raking a hand through his hair as he went. "Now go and choose a dress. Or send them all away. But don't come in here crying to me because you believe you've been cheated out of your little girl fantasy."

Tina sucked in a fortifying breath. She felt like a fool, and it wasn't a feeling she enjoyed. "It's not my fantasy," she told him angrily. It wasn't entirely true, since she and Lucia had often dreamed of their wedding day when they were teenagers, but she was quickly adjusting her expectations of what her adult life was going to bring her.

He looked thunderous. "*Maledizione!* Then why did you barge into my meeting as if someone had stolen your puppy?"

Chastened, Tina felt her anger crumple under the weight of embarrassment. She'd wanted to be taken seriously, and yet she couldn't manage not to storm into a business meeting because she'd been focused on her own hurt feelings. No wonder her brother didn't think she could handle the pressure of working for him.

"You didn't ask me what I wanted. You simply assumed," she told him. She took a halting step toward him, clasped her fist over her heart, which beat hard. She *wanted* him to understand. Needed him to understand.

"I'm a person, Nico. An individual with wants and needs of my own. I don't need to be told what to do. I want to be *asked* what I want."

He picked up a pen and tossed it down again. Then he sat at the desk and pushed both hands through his hair, resting his head in his palms. The move stunned her. "What do you want, Tina? What will make you happy?"

Her throat ached at that single gesture of defeat. Now she felt petty. How did he do that? How did he move her from blazing anger to embarrassment and then guilt in the space of a few seconds?

She realized that he must have gone to a lot of trouble to bring the gowns here. After all, they'd left Italy quickly and arrived in Gibraltar with no preparation.

He'd done something miraculous, something he'd not had to do but that he'd probably thought she might want. Tina's throat ached. Outside this room, a seamstress waited with several top designer gowns. All she had to do was choose one, and the woman would fit it to her body in the space of a few hours.

It was all too real, too fast. She swallowed hard. She didn't know what she was doing. She wasn't ready for any of this—and neither was he. They were like two people turned loose in a vast forest without a compass or a map. They were stumbling, fumbling and getting more and more lost.

And hurting each other in the process.

She knew what she wanted, what she wished she could do. It was impossible, but she said it anyway.

"I'd like to go back to that night in Venice and make a different choice," she whispered. For both their sakes.

He looked up, his eyes sharp, hard. "Clearly, that isn't going to happen. I suggest you find a way to be happy now."

If only she could.

* * *

Tina chose a gown. In the end, she'd been unable to send the seamstress or the dresses away. The one she picked was a gorgeous creation, a strapless gown that hugged her torso and then fell in a lush fall of voluminous fabric from her hips. The dress was unadorned, which was part of the reason it had appealed to her. The beauty of it was its simplicity.

She chose to wear her hair up, though she left it curly, and tucked in a few sprigs of tiny white daisies. The wedding was to take place in the hotel, so there was no need to worry about piling herself and the fabric into a car.

No, all she had to do was go downstairs at the appointed time and arrive at the small chapel the hotel had set up for the purpose. She'd chosen to walk down the aisle by herself, since Renzo was not here to give her away. She refused to allow one of Nico's security detail to do it though he had suggested it. When she'd declined, he'd shrugged.

Now she gathered the small bouquet of flowers the hotel had provided her while the woman who'd helped her dress sniffled.

"You look so lovely, miss," she said. "He will be so proud when he sees you."

Tina managed a smile. She didn't think Nico would be anything other than relieved to get this over with, but she didn't say so. "Thank you, Lisbeth."

Lisbeth dabbed her eyes with a tissue. "It's so romantic, isn't it? Your man flying all those gowns in to surprise you. I could have melted on the spot."

Tina's fingers shook as she twisted a curl that had fallen over her brow. Her stomach dived into the floor. He'd flown the gowns in special, and she'd reacted so furiously over it. She felt childish and hollow inside as she remembered him with his head in his hands.

It made her remember the younger him, oddly enough. He'd been different then. More human. She could picture him at their kitchen table, laughing with Renzo and her mother while she sat very quietly and tried not to blush or stammer or let her adoration of him show whenever she looked at him.

He was a harder man now. He wasn't vulnerable in the least, and yet he'd shown that single moment of emotional vulnerability. As if the weight of the things pressing down on him had, for a moment, been too much to bear.

She'd wanted to go to him and put her arms around him. She'd wanted to ask him to share his burdens with her, but she had known he would not. Now she was ashamed of herself. She'd been so focused on her own feelings that she'd failed to consider his.

He'd insisted they marry for the baby, but it couldn't be what he'd planned to do with his life. A family was such a life-changing decision; to have it forced upon you was not what *anyone* would wish for. It wasn't just about her feelings. It was about his, as well.

Tina left the suite and took the elevator down to the main level, Lisbeth making the trip with her in order to guide her to the right place. Nico was waiting for her outside the chapel. Tina nearly stumbled to a halt, but managed to keep walking anyway. It was just a superstition that it was bad luck for him to see her before the wedding—though how could it get any worse than a wedding neither of them truly wanted?

He was dark and forbidding in his tuxedo as he stood near the entrance. He looked so serious that her heart notched up. His gaze raked her, those stormy eyes smoldering with heat when he met hers again.

"Is something wrong?" she asked.

"There is one last thing we must do before we wed," he told her. He led her into a small adjoining room with a desk and chairs. The two men she'd seen with him this morning were there. With a jolt, she recognized them for what they were.

Lawyers.

If the serious expressions on their faces didn't give it away, then the briefcases and neat pile of papers would have. Nico handed her a pen as one of the lawyers pushed the papers toward her, which were conveniently flipped back for her signature.

And she'd actually felt a glimmering of sympathy for him earlier? Tina turned to look at him, anger kindling in her belly.

"Certain things must be spelled out before we marry, Tina," he said before she could speak.

"I am aware of that," she said tightly as she settled into a chair and jerked the papers from beneath the lawyer's fingers. A prenuptial agreement wasn't unusual or even unexpected. But there was something about the cold-blooded efficiency with which he'd orchestrated this entire marriage thus far that had her on edge.

Yes, he'd gone to a lot of trouble to get the gowns. And she'd actually felt badly that she'd been mad over what she'd considered to be his high-handedness—but now she was angry again. Angry because he'd waited until the last moment, when she was dressed and ready for the ceremony, to spring this on her.

No doubt because he expected her to sign without question. Because he thought she was empty-headed and in need of someone to tell her what to do. Maybe he expected her to simply do as she was told, which made him no better than Renzo in that respect.

She glanced up at him, the agreement in her hands, and hoped she looked coolly controlled. "You may want to sit down," she said. "This might take a while."

His lips twitched. She wasn't certain if it was annoyance or humor that caused it. Regardless, it only made her more determined.

"It is a fair agreement," he said. "You get quite a generous settlement should we divorce, and maintenance for life."

Tina flipped to the pages where the financial portion was spelled out. "Very generous," she said after she'd scanned the numbers. "And yet you've made a mistake." She tapped the pen against the page.

One of the lawyers cleared his throat, and Tina sliced her gaze in his direction. The look she gave him must have been quelling because he subsided without speaking.

"I believe that Pietro wanted to say there is no mistake," Nico said. She thought he sounded vaguely amused, but she was too irritated to be sure.

"Well, there is. You are forgetting that this sum—" she tapped the pen on the page again "—must be adjusted for inflation. A divorce in a year is quite a different animal than a divorce in twenty."

"So it is," Nico replied.

"You've also failed to take into account any money I may bring into the marriage."

"I don't want Renzo's money." His voice was harder this time.

Tina fixed him with an even stare. "I'm not talking about Renzo's money. I'm talking about mine."

One eyebrow lifted. "I wasn't aware you had any."

"I do, in fact," she told him evenly. "I've made investments of my own."

"I'm not interested in your petty investments," he snapped, and anger seared into her. Petty investments, indeed. She wasn't about to tell him what she'd accumulated, unless it became a point in the contract. Her wealth came nowhere close to his, or Renzo's, but she'd earned it herself through the strength of her skills—and she wasn't going to give him control over it.

"Great. Then you won't mind adding a clause that states that fact." How typically arrogant of him to assume that she brought nothing to the marriage other than what Renzo had given her.

Nico's eyes burned hot as he took the pen from her and bent over the papers. He crossed out the figure that was written there and substantially increased it. And then he flipped to the end and added a clause about any money she brought into the marriage.

The first lawyer took the page and read it, then handed it back with a nod.

"Satisfied?" Nico asked as he shoved the document toward her again.

"I'll let you know once I've read the whole thing."

It took over twenty minutes, but she finished reading and attached her signature in bold strokes. She'd worked hard on that signature, ever since Frau Decker had told her she wrote like a mouse that expected to be eaten by the cat at any minute.

"Grazie, cara," Nico said, taking her hand in his and helping her from the chair. A frisson of excitement rolled through her at his slight touch. How very annoying in light of what had just happened.

He lifted her hand to his mouth, as if he knew how she reacted to him, and pressed his lips lightly to her skin. A tingle shot down her spine. "Now, let us get married."

Tina forced a smile. "Yes, let's."

She might be a mouse, and Nico might be the big cat waiting to pounce on her—but she fully intended to choke him on the way down.

They returned to Italy as soon as the ceremony was over. Nico thought about staying in Gibraltar for the night, but he had urgent business to attend to and no time for dallying.

He could hardly credit that he was a married man now. It wasn't something he'd expected to do anytime soon, if ever. Not even to preserve the title within his direct line. It would have gone to a cousin, so it would not have been lost to the family, and that would have been good enough for him.

But now he was married, and to the most unlikely woman of all. Tina sat across from him as the jet winged its way back to Italy. She was still in her gown because he'd insisted on leaving immediately. He'd expected her to change on the plane, but she had not made a move to do so. She simply sat and read her eReader, as if flying in a wedding gown was the most ordinary thing imaginable.

She looked, he had to admit, incredible. Her riot of hair was contained in an elegant loose twist, though several strands had come free to frame her face, with its pert nose and long lashes that made her eyes look as if they were closed when they were merely downcast and concentrating on her book.

Her shoulders were bare, and her breasts rose into lush, golden mounds that threatened to spill over the stiff bodice. He remembered kissing her this afternoon, when she'd burst into the office in that ridiculously small bikini, and his body grew hard.

It had taken everything he'd had not to untie her bikini bottoms and thrust into her right there up against the door. He'd been about to do just that when the noise had reminded him they were not truly alone.

Nico shifted in his seat, unable to concentrate on the spreadsheets before him. He closed the computer with a snap, and Tina glanced up. Need jolted through him as their eyes clashed and held. He could feel the tension in the air, the electric snap of sexual promise that flowed between them like water gushing over a fall.

It would be so good when he stripped her naked again. So, so good.

"Why did you not change into something more comfortable?" he asked her.

She shrugged a pretty shoulder. "You can be forgiven for not knowing it, I suppose, but wedding gowns require a bit of help to get into and out of."

He didn't think his body could get any harder. Apparently, he was wrong.

"I'll help," he said. Growled, really.

Her violet eyes were wide. And blazing, he realized. As if she, too, were doing everything she could to not think about sex and failing miserably.

"I'm not sure you wouldn't tear the fabric," she murmured.

"I might," he said, his blood beating hot and fierce in his veins. Urging him to take her.

"I'd rather you didn't. If we have a daughter, I might like to give this dress to her someday."

A fierce wave of possession swept him then. Why did the prospect of a child cause his gut to clench and his heart to throb?

"And if I promised to be careful?"

Her tongue darted over her pink lower lip; in response, the pain in his groin shifted to an excruciating level.

"I might have to accept your offer, since there is no other way to get out of the dress."

Dear God, he wanted her right now. He wanted to take her hand and lead her to the plane's bedroom and have his wicked way with her.

But they'd been airborne for an hour already and he knew they weren't far from landing. Besides, he wanted far more than a quick tumble from her. He wanted to explore her thoroughly. He wanted to strip her slowly and build her excitement until she begged him to possess her. And that would take time. Time he did not have right now.

There was no choice but to control this need raging inside him like a hurricane.

"I will take you up on that, Tina, but not until we are safely home again."

She dipped her head, but not before he thought she looked somewhat disappointed. The knowledge she wanted him, too, sent a slice of raw lust burrowing deep into his gut. When he'd taken her to bed in Venice, he'd thought she would be like other women. And she had been, until the moment when he'd realized he couldn't quite forget the sexy virgin siren he'd bedded that night.

What was it about her? He'd been asking himself that since the morning after their encounter in Venice.

If he'd known who she was, he wouldn't have touched her, regardless that doing so would anger Renzo. He might be bad, but he wasn't that bad. Or, he was that bad, but he wouldn't have been able to do it when he remembered her as a shy teenager, hiding behind her hair and gazing at him with puppy dog eyes when she thought he wasn't looking.

She'd been sweet, shy and so very innocent. Her adoration had amused him at the time, though he'd been careful not to let her know that he knew how she felt.

She didn't gaze at him that way any longer, and he found he missed it in a perverse sort of way. She'd worshipped him once, and now she did not. Now she looked cool and almost indifferent at times. He was certain, however, that she was not.

"What are you reading so intensely?" he asked, determined to change the subject in an effort to get himself under control.

She looked down at the eReader as if she'd forgotten it existed. What she said next was not even close to what he'd expected her to say. "Oh, just a journal article on rational option pricing and derivative investment instruments."

Nico blinked as he dredged up memories of university. "You're reading about financial engineering?"

He should have realized there was more inside that lovely head than he'd assumed, considering the way she'd gone after the financial arrangements in the prenup. She'd been a tiger. He'd thought she was just very savvy, but now he realized it was something entirely different.

It turned him on in ways he hadn't imagined. And it made him wonder about those investments she'd mentioned. Not because he thought she'd made a fortune, but because he was suddenly curious.

She looked fierce. "And why is that so hard to believe? Not that you've ever asked, but I have a degree in finance. With honors, I might add."

No, he hadn't asked. Why hadn't he asked? Because

he'd thought her expertise was in shopping and look-ing pretty, that's why. It was the sort of thing he was accustomed to from the women in his life. Not that he didn't have seriously smart women working for him, but he'd never actually dated any of them.

"That's impressive," he told her sincerely. "I'm sur-prised you aren't working for your brother with that kind of résumé."

She looked angry. "Yes, well, Renzo has certain opinions about what I should be doing. And working for him was not it."

"Then he is a fool."

Her eyes were suddenly sharp. "Really? Does that mean you'd consider allowing your wife to work in the finance department of Gavretti Manufacturing?"

He flicked an imaginary speck of lint from his tux-edo. "Perhaps. One day." He had no intention of letting her anywhere near his financial department. She was a D'Angeli, and he didn't kid himself that her loyalties had suddenly switched when she'd said her vows.

Still, if he'd been Renzo, he would have used her ex-pertise. He could say that honestly. He always used the best tool for the job.

"I suppose I can't ask for a better answer," she said. Then she laughed, the sound so light and beautiful that it pierced him in unexpected ways. "I bet you thought I'd tell you I was reading a romance novel, or perhaps a tome that everyone claims to have read but really haven't."

He couldn't help but smile in return. She was infec-tious when she laughed. "Such as?"

"Oh, *Ulysses* maybe. Or *Moby-Dick*. Something giant and meaty and excruciating in the extreme."

Nico put a hand over his heart in mock horror. "I happen to like *Ulysses.*"

The corners of her mouth trembled as she worked to keep a straight face. "Then I am sorry for disparaging it. I'm sure it's a fine piece of literature."

"You aren't sorry," he said, enjoying the way her face lit up with mischief.

She gave up the pretense and laughed again. "No, not really."

"Don't worry," he told her. "I've never actually read *Ulysses.* I was just teasing you."

She shook her head. "That's very bad of you."

He took her hand in his, his thumb ghosting over her palm. He could feel the tremor that ran through her body. An answering thrill cascaded within him. Soon, he would take her. He had to.

"I like being bad," he murmured as he nibbled her pretty fingers. "I excel at it, in fact."

Her only answer was another shiver.

CHAPTER NINE

TINA was on edge in a way she hadn't been since the night she'd met Nico in Venice. That night, when she'd gotten into the gondola with the enigmatic stranger, she'd known they would end up in bed together even if she hadn't fully admitted it to herself.

Tonight, she was admitting it. And she wanted it so desperately her skin tingled with anticipation. It didn't matter that she'd been furious and hurt earlier. Nothing mattered except that she'd stood in that tiny chapel and promised to love, honor and cherish until death do us part, while her heart thrummed and her palms sweated and the man standing beside her gazed at her with piercing silver eyes.

They were in this together now, officially, and tonight was their wedding night. She couldn't quite wrap her head around it. She was a married woman, the marchesa di Casari, and her family had no idea. Guilt slid deep into her bones. Renzo would hit the roof when he found out. Thank God that wouldn't be for another couple of weeks at least—more if she was lucky. Still, she had time to figure out how to tell everyone what she'd done.

And time to get to the root of the problem between Renzo and Nico. If she could just understand that, she could help to fix this thing between them. She didn't expect they would be best friends ever again, but if they could at least be in the same room together without wanting to kill each other, that would be a start.

The plane had landed half an hour ago now. She'd thought they were returning to Castello di Casari, but instead they were in Rome. She expected that Nico had a huge villa somewhere in the city, but rather it was an exclusive apartment overlooking the ancient rooftops and splendid ruins.

There was no staff waiting to greet them, no Giuseppe with his kind smile and brisk efficiency. There was only Nico, and the lights of Rome spread out like a carpet of fireflies.

She felt suddenly awkward as she stood in the darkened living room and watched Nico prowling toward her, his dark good looks emphasized by the formality of the tuxedo. He'd undone his tie a while ago, and unbuttoned the top couple of buttons of his shirt to give a tantalizing glimpse of bronzed skin.

She focused on that slice of skin until he stopped in front of her and her eyes drifted up to meet his. It jolted her again just how very handsome he was, with those piercing eyes and perfect cheekbones.

He took her hand in his without breaking eye contact, placed it on his shoulder.

Then he did the same with the other one, placing it on his opposite shoulder as her heart thrummed and her body warmed to dangerous temperatures.

"Alone at last," he told her with a wicked smile that made hunger slide into her veins.

"So it would seem."

"I want you, Tina," he said, dipping his head to place a soft kiss on her cheek. She closed her eyes and tilted her head back as his mouth traced a path along her jaw and down the column of her throat. "Too much," he murmured against her skin, and the vibration of his voice dripped into her bloodstream like pure adrenaline. "I've thought of nothing but this for hours now."

A thrill rocketed through her. "I should tell you no," she said on a little half gasp as his lips found the sweet spot behind her ear.

"It's inevitable, *bella*. You want me as I want you."

"I might," she admitted. "But I'm not exactly thrilled with how you've treated me."

He lifted his head to look at her. "The prenup was necessary. You know that."

She shrugged, but she didn't remove her hands from his shoulders. "I do know. But you could have picked a better time."

He sighed, his palms sliding along her hips. "It wasn't ready before then. It takes time to put together a document of that size."

"I realize that, Nico. I'm not stupid. But you could have told me earlier that we'd be dealing with it at some point."

He dipped his head and ran his mouth along the column of her throat while she tried not to moan or fall apart in his arms. "I'm sorry," he said. "I should have mentioned it."

She sighed. She had an apology of her own to make. "Thank you for getting the dresses. It was nice of you."

His hands slipped around to cup her bottom. "I thought you were angry over that."

Tina swallowed as heat swirled inside her belly. "I was. But I realize you were trying to be nice. You just went about it in a typical male fashion."

He pulled back to look down at her. "A typical male fashion?"

She nodded as she gazed up at him. "Yes. You assumed I would be happy so you proceeded without consulting me."

"And you would prefer I consult you in the future about decisions of this nature?"

"About decisions that involve me. Yes."

He dipped his head and ran his tongue along the top of her bodice. "And what about this, Tina? Do you wish to continue? Or shall we say good-night here?"

"Nico," she breathed.

"You have the power to say no," he told her. "I want only a willing wife in my bed."

Tina shuddered as he pulled her against him, the evidence of his need for her pressing into her abdomen. He was hard, ready, and liquid heat slid through her in response.

"I think I'm ready," she said, a shiver running through her because he'd asked. *He'd asked.*

"Think? Or know? Because I don't want any ambiguity, *cara.* Choose me now, or go to bed alone."

He was truly asking what she wanted—and she was a goner.

"I know. I *know.*" Tina wrapped her arms around his neck at the same moment his mouth sought hers, capturing it in a kiss so scorching she nearly melted from the heat. She moaned when he slid his tongue against hers, and her knees suddenly felt as if they were made of water.

She was hot and ready, like a pot that had been on the burner all day—and Nico seemed to know it.

Her pulse thrummed in her ears, her throat, her breastbone, pounding out a beat that made her dizzy while his tongue licked into her with such devastating skill that all she could do was cling to him.

He made her feel so much. So many conflicting emotions crashing through her along with a healthy, hungry appetite for what they were about to do. How could she want him so acutely? And how could he be so very bad for her at the same time?

Nico pulled her hips against his again, until she could once more feel the evidence of an impressive erection.

Tina whimpered. Just like that, it was suddenly too much to wait even a minute more. She'd decided to do this thing, and there was no going back.

She ripped at the studs holding his shirt closed until he laughed deep in his throat and shrugged out of his jacket, letting it fall where he stood. Then his hands came over hers, helped her tear the shirt open as studs popped and flew.

Her hands were suddenly on his hot flesh, her palms sliding along his skin, learning the texture of him once more. He was so hot, so hard and muscular, and she wanted him naked before another minute passed. She couldn't think about anything but him. He drove her crazy with need.

She tugged the shirt from his trousers and then went after his belt and zipper while Nico fumbled with the buttons at her back. She could feel his frustration mounting with the tiny buttons.

He broke the kiss and turned her in his arms. "Don't rip them," she gasped.

"I won't." His voice was clipped, rough, and it made her tremble. Soon the bodice began to loosen, but he lost patience and turned her again, pulling the front of the gown down just enough so that her breasts spilled freely into his hands. Her nipples were hard little points that he flicked with his thumbs while a deep shiver rolled through her.

"*Dio*, you are so beautiful."

A skein of pleasure uncoiled in her belly, along with the bone-deep need that made her sex ache. Niccolo Gavretti had said she was beautiful. Nico, the notorious playboy, the man she'd mooned after as a love-struck teenager, had just said she was beautiful. It was a dream come true in some ways.

She wanted to tell him that he was beautiful, too, but his mouth captured hers again, driving all thoughts from her head except one: *need you now*.

His mouth was questing, demanding, and she responded in kind, her heart hammering, her skin on fire as she tried to get closer to him. He gathered fistfuls of her skirts, shoved them up her hips so he could hook his fingers into her panties and push them down until gravity took over and they fell to her feet.

Tina was never so glad she'd not worn garters as she was at that moment. "Now, Nico," she said against his lips. "Now."

He guided her backward until she bumped into something. Before she could tell what it was, he lifted her and sat her down on a table. She was so focused on him that she had no idea where they were—dining room, kitchen, living room—and she didn't care. All she cared about was this man and this moment.

Tina wrapped her legs around him as he pushed her thighs open and stepped between them. His hands were on her hips, holding her in place as their mouths fused again and again, their kisses drunken and hot and utterly addictive. She fumbled with his zipper, jerked it down with shaky fingers. And then her hands were in his trousers, freeing him.

He groaned as she wrapped her hand around him, slid her palm along his hot, velvety shaft. He shoved her skirts higher and pulled her hands away from his body. She made a sound of disappointment, but a moment later she felt the blunt head of his penis pressing into her and every last thought flew out of her mind.

He cupped her bottom, tilting her backward slightly before he thrust deeply inside her—it wasn't a sudden movement, but it was overpowering in its intensity. One moment she was craving him, the next he'd filled her. Tina cried out in surprise and pleasure, and his entire body stilled.

"Have I hurt you?" His voice was rough.

Yes, she wanted to say. *Yes.*

But the pain wasn't physical. "No. Please don't stop."

His laugh was ragged. "Stop? Not possible, *tesoro.* Not possible." He leaned forward and kissed her again, and she could feel his body pulsing inside hers. Had it been this exciting the first time? Had she wanted him so desperately that she'd been willing to do anything to have him?

Possibly, but it didn't matter. *This* was what mattered. Now, when he was inside her, his entire being focused on her. He was the kind of man who knew how to make a woman's body sing, and she knew this night would be even better than the first because she wasn't as naive as before. Because she knew what to expect—and she craved it.

Craved him.

Tina didn't want to let him go, as if she would wake up and find it had all been a dream if she did. She wrapped her arms around his neck, her body bending into him as he began to move. Their tongues tangled as he stroked into her with such skill she wanted to weep.

She knew he tried to be gentle, but it wasn't really possible.

For either of them. They were joined together with no barriers between them this time—and they'd waited for two long months to be in this place again, though they did not know it was what they'd been waiting for.

Nico pushed her back until she was supporting herself on her hands, her back arching, her breasts thrusting into the air for his pleasure. His lips closed over an aroused nipple, spiking the pleasure within her until she wasn't certain she could hold out another second.

"Nico," she gasped, her senses filled with him.

Deep within her, the explosion began to build. His lovemaking was raw, powerful, almost desperate, as if he'd held back for far too long and even now perched on the edge of his control. His fingers dug into her hips as he held her hard and drove into her.

Tina dragged her eyes open to look at him, to look at the picture they made. He bent over her body, the ruins of his shirt clinging to his broad shoulders. His skin glistened with moisture and she lifted a hand to rake it through his hair. He dragged his mouth across her breasts then, his lips closing around her other nipple. Tina clasped his head to her with a soft moan, loving the sharp, sweet spike of pleasure that tugged at her. Her breasts were so much more sensitive than they'd been only a few weeks ago, and she cried out as his tongue swirled and teased and tormented.

He drove her relentlessly, almost savagely, until she shattered with a sharp cry, her entire body clenching with the force of her orgasm. Her legs tightened around him, as if she was afraid he might try to leave her.

But he didn't leave. And he didn't stop, gripping her

buttocks in his hands and lifting her to him until the new angle made her breath catch once more.

"Again," he said, the muscles in his neck and chest and abdomen corded tight as he held her up and drove into her.

Tina lay back on the table, her arms over her head in helpless surrender, her eyes closed as she pushed her hips up to meet him. She was a creature of pleasure now, a being who existed for this alone. He came down on top of her, the fabric of her dress rustling, no doubt wrinkling hopelessly.

She didn't care.

He dominated her with the strength of his body, and she wrapped her legs high around his back, tears squeezing from her closed eyes to leak down her temples and into her hair.

It was too beautiful, too perfect to be with him like this. He destroyed her. And she was far happier than she should be.

"Tina," he groaned. "*Dio*, don't cry."

He threaded his fingers through hers, his mouth seeking hers once more. He kissed her far more sweetly than she'd thought he was capable of at that moment. Fear swirled in her belly then. Everything about being with him felt right—but did he feel it, too, or was this simply the consummate ladies' man doing what he did best?

Tina squeezed her eyes tighter. She couldn't think like that. She simply couldn't. They were married now and they had a child on the way. He was hers.

And, oh, God, that's just what she'd wanted, wasn't it? She wanted him to belong to her—had from the first moment he'd walked into their tiny kitchen with Renzo and smiled at her. He'd been so strong and handsome and perfect—and she'd been shy, awkward and unworthy of ever getting such a man, even in her wildest dreams.

He raised his head, as if he sensed the turmoil in her heart. "You're thinking too much," he said gruffly. "Stop thinking."

And then he made it impossible for her to think as he thrust into her again and again, harder and harder, until she caught fire, until her body shattered in a million bright shards of color and her breath tore from her in a long, broken cry.

She was still gasping and reeling when he followed her into oblivion, holding her tightly to him, his hips grinding into her one last time as a deep shudder racked him.

Her heart throbbed in the silence, filling her ears with the sound of her blood rushing through her sensitized body. Tina put her hand in his hair, held him to her as he buried his face against her neck. His hair was damp, hot, and his breath ghosted over her heated skin, cooling her.

She gazed up at the ceiling, dazed by what had just happened between them. She was still in her wedding gown—her very crumpled wedding gown—and lying on a long table. A console table, she realized. They hadn't even made it out of the living room.

She'd married someone her family hated and now she was having wild sex with him on a table. She ought to be ashamed—and yet she wasn't. She was thrilled at the illicitness of their encounter.

He wasn't a bad man, she told herself. He wanted what was best for the baby, the same as she did, and he'd flown wedding dresses in for her so she wouldn't have to get married in something that she'd worn to lunch or shopping with Mama and Lucia. He'd tried to make sure she had something special. That didn't make him good by a long shot, but it made him human at least.

She was still breathing hard when he pushed off her and turned to tuck himself away. A frisson of alarm crept through her then. They'd had sex and he was done. He would leave her while he went to work on his laptop, or maybe he'd leave the apartment and go into the city and not come back until she'd fallen asleep waiting for him to return.

He caught her gaze then and quirked an eyebrow. "I'm not leaving, Tina."

She hated that he knew what she was thinking simply from looking at her—and yet she was relieved, too.

"I hope not," she told him, pushing herself up on her elbows. "I was quite enjoying that."

Nico's gaze was sharp and hot as he smoothed her gown down before he helped her to stand. Her legs were wobbly and she swayed into him. He caught her close, his fingers burning into the exposed skin of her back.

His smile scorched her. "We definitely aren't finished yet," he told her, tucking a lock of hair behind her ear. "That was merely a prelude."

Tina's heart was still racing. "Some prelude."

He kissed her. In spite of everything that had just happened, in spite of the fact she was spent, excitement blossomed in her belly, kindling like a flash fire.

"You haven't seen anything yet," he promised.

Nico lay in the dark and listened to the breathing of the woman beside him. She'd fallen into an exhausted sleep hours ago, but his mind wouldn't quiet enough to let him do the same. His body was replete, drunk on sex and high on the endorphins a good release could bring—and yet, if she turned to him now and ran a soft hand over his thigh, he'd harden in an instant.

And that was what he didn't quite understand. What was this nearly insatiable need for her?

Oh, he loved sex and women, and he'd been known to spend long nights making love to whichever woman had caught his fancy. That was not unusual in the least. Nor was the fact she was beside him in the bed. He didn't mistake sex and sleeping for love, and he made sure the women he was with knew that.

He knew that some men left in the middle of the night, or made the woman leave, but what was the sense in that? If he woke up aroused, he wanted a soft female body in which to spend himself.

No, he didn't leave in the middle of the night like a vampire, and he didn't kick a woman out of bed until he tired of her. How quickly that happened depended entirely upon her.

The instant the games began—the jealousy, the pouting, the efforts to make him say that he was beginning to feel something more—she was gone.

But now he had a wife, and that wife intrigued him more than he could remember being intrigued in quite a while. His life, while full of beautiful women and all the finer things money could buy, had left him empty of late. More lonely than content, more restless than happy.

Tina, however, excited him again. He'd been so hot for her that he'd taken her on a table in the living room with the lights of Rome stretched out below. He should have made it more special for her, but he'd been unable to wait. She'd asked him not to ruin her dress—he hadn't, but he'd damn sure creased it. After that first frantic coupling, he'd carried her to the bedroom and taken the time he should have taken initially. He'd explored her, aroused her, and satisfied her over and over.

He loved the sounds she made when she came, the way she said his name, her soft voice breaking at the end as if he were the one thing she needed in this world to survive. It was a plea, each and every time—and yet it wasn't. He sensed there was something about her he could not touch, and it drove him crazy wondering what that was.

Did she purposely hold a part of herself back? Or was he imagining things?

He turned in the bed and slid a hand along her hip before pulling her into the curve of his body. She felt good there, and he lay beside her and just listened to her breathing.

Valentina D'Angeli. *Valentina Gavretti*, he corrected fiercely.

How was it that he lay here with Renzo's little sister and the only thing he felt was protective? He should feel triumphant, as if he'd finally found the way to get beneath Renzo's skin—but he didn't.

She turned in his arms then, her hand coming to rest on his cheek. It made him feel fierce inside. If Renzo tried to take her away...

"Nico," she sighed.

"Yes, *cara*?"

He could see her smile in the dark. "Nothing."

His body was already reacting though he tried to think of something other than sex. But his penis was throbbing to life regardless. Sometimes it definitely had a will of its own. He did not doubt that women were right when they accused men of thinking with their genitalia.

He pushed a lock of curly hair out of her face. "Tell me something, Tina."

"What's that," she asked sleepily, burrowing into him even more.

"I don't understand how you were still a virgin." He'd been thinking about it since she'd blasted back into his life. She was so passionate, so honest and open in her sexuality, that it didn't make sense. She burned him up with her heat, and he craved more of the same—had since the first night he'd been with her.

She shrugged. "I never found anyone I wanted to be with."

He'd never claimed to understand women's minds, so he didn't argue the point. To her, it made perfect sense. "Then why did you choose me?"

"Actually, I chose someone else," she said, and he couldn't stop the slice of jealousy that slammed through him. "But he smelled like garlic. You didn't."

Nico blinked. "You mean it came down to garlic?"

She nodded. "Yep. Garlic. One really shouldn't eat garlic if one expects to seduce a woman."

He couldn't help but laugh at that. "Then I suppose I should be grateful I skipped the garlic."

She tilted her head back on the pillow to look at him. He could feel the intensity of her gaze, even if he couldn't actually see what was in her eyes in the dark. "Do you really mean that?"

Everything inside him grew still. He didn't know what he meant, but he wanted to tell her not to read too much into it, though he knew that she already had. She was young and naive, at least as far as relationships went, and he couldn't tell her the truth right now. He couldn't tell her that he didn't believe in love between a man and a woman. He only believed in sexual chemistry—which they had an abundance of—and that usually fizzled after a while.

Except nothing was fizzling at the moment.

"I don't regret being your first lover, Tina." That was most definitely true. He shifted his pelvis so she could feel the evidence of his continuing need for her.

"Oh," she said, her voice husky. And yet he sensed she was somehow disappointed in his answer. Was it because of the baby? Or because she hoped there could be something more between them than simple lust?

He didn't know, and he didn't want to ask. He didn't want to talk about expectations, or about what he thought might happen when they tired of each other. It was too soon, and he was still growing accustomed to the idea of a wife.

He wouldn't allow this to disintegrate to the point it harmed their child, but he knew they would have to address it one day. What happened when they were ready to go their separate ways?

"Go to sleep, Tina," he told her somewhat gruffly. He was aroused, but he'd get over it. "You need your rest."

She made a disapproving sound. "And if I don't want to sleep?"

He didn't think he could grow any harder than he was in that moment. "What do you want, *tesoro*?"

"I think you know."

He gathered her closer, nuzzled the hair at her temple. "Can I possibly be so lucky?"

She slid a hand over his hip. "Enjoy it while you can. I imagine things will change once this baby really starts to grow."

She pressed her mouth to his chest, her tongue swirling against his skin as she wrapped her fingers around him and squeezed.

"Tell me what you want," he said—groaned, really. He didn't expect her to push him onto his back and straddle him, but he was damned happy she did. He groaned again as she sank down on top of him. Her movements were slow at first, inexpert, but they increased in tempo until he didn't care about anything but what she did to him. He gripped her hips and thrust up into her while she gasped and moaned. When she stiffened and choked out his name, he came in a hot rush that left him gasping and spent.

"That was lovely," she said huskily. Then she leaned down and kissed him slowly, clearly pleased with herself. His heart tapped an insane rhythm in his chest as he lay beneath her and concentrated on breathing evenly. "Really lovely.

"And, Nico," she added when he was still trying to catch his breath and couldn't manage to say a word. "I'm glad you were my first, too."

A stab of unexpected emotion pierced him as he keyed in on one word. *First*.

First implied there would be a second. It twisted his gut into knots.

Chemistry, he told himself, as he closed his eyes and hugged her to him. It was only chemistry that made him want to punch something at the thought of her with another man.

CHAPTER TEN

THEY spent the next few days in Rome while Nico attended to business. During the day, he went to meetings, worked on his computer at home or had long conference calls in his home office.

But at night, he was hers. Tina shivered to think about what happened at night. And sometimes during the day, when he came home early or ended a call and came back inside to find her on her computer or reading.

She'd thought that sex couldn't get any more exciting or amazing than it already was.

She'd been wrong. When he turned to her in the night and slid a palm along her hip, she shuddered, her body coming alive with sensation. And then she melted into him, fusing herself to him, taking him deep inside her and losing herself in the rightness of it.

He owned her body, and he knew it. Whether she straddled him and rode him frantically or whether he made love to her with his mouth before filling her with that part of him she craved, it didn't matter. He owned her as surely as if he'd taken a brand and seared his name into her skin.

It was…shocking. And frightening. How could she need him so much in such a short space of time?

"Hello, earth to Tina. Yoo-hoo."

Tina focused on Lucia, who sat across from her in the restaurant and waved her hand back and forth in front of Tina's face.

"I'm sorry," Tina said, smiling at her friend as she picked up her water glass and took a sip. "Just thinking."

Lucia made a face. "I can guess what about. That man is simply gorgeous, and you are one lucky girl."

"There's more to a marriage than having a gorgeous man," Tina said wryly. She'd told Lucia everything, even the part about their hasty marriage in Gibraltar. Rather than being horrified, Lucia was giddy, as if they were still sixteen and sneaking cigarettes in the janitor's closet. Tina shook her head. She'd hated cigarettes, and hated the sick feeling she got whenever she sneaked around.

She had that feeling today, in the pit of her stomach, as she thought about Renzo and Mama. Soon, she would have to tell them what she'd done.

"Oh, I'm sure." Lucia lifted her glass. "But it doesn't hurt a bit, I'll bet." She took a sip before putting the glass down again and leaning forward. "So tell me if his nickname is well earned. Is he Naughty Niccolo in the bedroom as well as on the track?"

Tina colored. "Lucia, I don't think—"

Lucia sat back again and blinked. "Don't tell me you've fallen in love with him. Tina, he's not the sort of man you love."

"No, of course not." She would be crazy to love him. She knew that.

And she *didn't*. How could she? They'd been together a week, and sex was not enough to base such a strong emotion on. Of course she'd thought she'd loved him once long ago, but she'd been a kid. She knew better now. Desperately wanting someone because they seemed out of reach, because they were gorgeous and kind to you and took your breath away with a smile was not love. It was infatuation.

She'd definitely been infatuated with him.

Tina waved a hand as if it were the silliest thing ever. "I'm pregnant, not stupid."

Lucia stabbed her salad. "I still don't know why you married him. You don't have to marry a man just because you get pregnant anymore. You also don't have to have the baby," she added.

Tina told herself not to get angry. Lucia was only speaking the truth, and she was the best friend Tina had ever had. She was not saying that Tina should get rid of her baby, just that it had been an option *if she'd wanted it.* Which she did not.

"I know that. But I want this baby. And Nico was rather insistent once I told him."

"I suppose he would be with the title and all." She dropped her fork, her eyes widening. "My God, I've just realized this means you are a marchesa now. Wouldn't the girls back at St. Katherine's be surprised!"

Tina laughed. "Disbelieving is more like it."

"Thank God those days are over." Lucia sighed.

"Definitely," Tina agreed, and put a hand over her belly beneath the table. Her stomach was still relatively flat, but it wouldn't be for much longer. "And you can rest assured I won't be sending this little one away to that awful place. Or any boarding school."

Lucia grinned again. "I just can't believe you're going to be a mother! I'm happy for you—but, Tina, what an amazing thing. The odds of that happening on your first time must be one in a zillion."

"Or more."

"Are you scared?" Lucia looked very serious then, and Tina reached over and clasped her hand, squeezing.

"No, actually. I'm learning a lot about being pregnant." The morning after she and Nico had arrived in Rome, she'd awakened to find him on his laptop in bed. When she'd stirred, he'd turned the computer to where she could see it.

"Look, *cara*, this is the site I was telling you about. You can join and track your pregnancy. There are articles, discussion groups and a bullctin board." He'd tapped a key, his eyes rapt on the screen. "So much to learn."

It still caused a pinch in her heart when she thought of the look on his face. How could she think he didn't care about her when he did things like that? It was true they never talked about feelings—but he *must* feel something. Mustn't he?

"When are you going to tell your mother and Renzo? They have a right to know, Tina."

Tina leaned back in her chair and sighed. "I know." It was the thorn in her happiness, the idea that she'd betrayed her family by marrying Nico. If they hadn't been half a world away, what would have happened?

She expected the news to hit the tabloids any day now, but she hoped that Renzo and Faith were so busy in the Caribbean that they weren't paying attention to gossip. She *would* tell them, but when she was ready.

After lunch, she and Lucia did a bit of shopping, and then Tina said goodbye and climbed into the chauffeured car that Nico insisted take her everywhere. She even had bodyguards, which she found slightly ridiculous, but two men in dark suits and headsets shadowed her every move now, though they traveled separately and never intruded.

Except for that one time when the crowds and hawkers around the Spanish Steps had been a bit boisterous. The man who'd shoved a rose in her face and wouldn't leave, even when she said no, had been jerked away and thrust in another direction.

Lucia hadn't even noticed, and their afternoon had continued pleasantly enough. But now Tina was tired and happy to return to the apartment. She almost wished they were back at Castello di Casari, with the sun and the water and the lovely garden, where she could lie underneath the pergola and dream.

And check her stock portfolio. She loved the thrill she got whenever she made a successful trade, when she watched the balance on her portfolio climb yet again because she'd taken a risk no one else had seen and it paid off.

Dammit, she was good at numbers and calculations. Very good. And Renzo didn't know it. Wouldn't have acknowledged it if he had, she thought sourly. It was a matter of pride for him that the women in his family didn't work after a lifetime of struggling to make ends meet—though Faith had certainly challenged that assumption quite successfully.

What would Nico think? He'd said he would consider letting her work for him, but she didn't imagine he would do so anytime soon. More likely, he'd said it to appease her because he'd made no mention of it since the plane ride back from Gibraltar.

When she let herself into the apartment, she could hear Nico's voice coming from the open door to his home office. He did not sound happy and she stopped, unsure whether to turn around and leave again until he was finished or to let him know she was home.

But the cold tone of his voice with its underlying hint

of despair had her moving forward until she stopped in the living area, her heart pounding in her throat. Her progress ceased when she heard a woman's voice.

The woman sounded haughty. She had the cultured tones of an aristocrat, and she seemed very angry. It took Tina a moment to realize that her voice was coming from the speakerphone.

"You are an ungrateful son, Niccolo," she snapped. "I sacrificed everything I had for you."

"What did you sacrifice, mother? As I recall, it was very little."

She sniffed. "You're just like your father. You don't care about me at all. You took his side against me. You always did."

"I did not," Nico growled. "I was a child. I had no idea who was right or who was wrong. But I knew one thing, and that was that neither of you seemed to want me around."

"It was difficult," his mother said after a long silence. "We pretended for your sake until you went to school. There was little point in it afterward."

"Yes, and when I begged to be allowed to come home, you were always unavailable for some reason or other. Traveling abroad or checking into a spa. How difficult life was for you, Mother."

Tina's heart ached to hear him sound so bitter. And she ached for the little boy he must have been, so lonely and unwanted. How cruel this woman was! And how Tina wanted to wrap her hands around his mother's neck and squeeze. What kind of mother did that to her child?

"It is difficult now," she said. "I put up with your father's philandering for years. The humiliation. But I always knew I would be taken care of in my old age.

And now you have inherited and I'm begging for alms at your feet."

"You are not a beggar," Nico said, his voice a harsh growl full of emotion that stunned her with its intensity. "You have a very generous allowance, and you will live within your means from now on. I will not allow the Gavretti holdings to be siphoned off and sold piecemeal in order to gratify your urges."

"That is ridiculous," she said. "There is no danger of that. You are simply a cruel and ungrateful son who would see his mother suffer rather than take care of her needs."

"It's time this conversation was over," Nico said.

"But I'm not finished—"

"I am."

His mother didn't speak again, and Tina knew he must have hung up on her. She walked to the entrance of the office, a lump in her throat. How awful it must have been to grow up with a woman like that, a woman who'd had no warmth for her child. Tina may not have known her father, but her mother was the most effusive and lovely person on the planet.

Mama had done everything possible to keep her and Renzo fed and clothed and happy. The only harsh words in their home came when someone was upset or angry over something—but they were gone quickly, and everyone was happy again. Tina had never felt like a burden to her mother, even when she probably had been at times.

Nico sat with his head in his hands and her heart squeezed hard at the sight of him like that. He looked defeated, the weight of his worries pressing down hard on those strong shoulders.

Something twisted inside her then, something

that stole her breath and made her stomach sink into her toes. She stood there as a maelstrom of emotion whipped her in its currents. Everything she had within her wanted to go to him and put her arms around him. To hold him tight and tell him that someone loved him even if his mother did not.

Tina pressed her hand to her mouth. She'd just told herself all the reasons why she did not love him. And yet none of them made sense any longer. Not in light of the feeling swelling in her heart.

But it couldn't be love. *Sympathy*. Yes, it had to be sympathy. She couldn't bear to see him hurting like this, and it made her want to hold him close and soothe him.

She must have made a sound, a sniffle as she tried to keep from letting any of the tears welling in her eyes fall, because he looked up, his dark gaze clashing with hers.

"I didn't know you were home," she said lamely, her body trembling with the force of the feelings whipping through her. She felt as though she'd tumbled over the edge of a cliff and there was no going back. She couldn't seem to find her equilibrium.

He pushed to his feet and shoved his hands in his pockets. He looked uncomfortable, restless. "I finished my meetings early."

She wanted to reach out to him, take him in her arms. But she didn't think he would welcome it. She tried to smile as if everything were normal. As if her heart weren't breaking for him.

"I went to lunch with my friend Lucia. It was nice to get out for a while."

The look on his face told her that she probably shouldn't have added that last bit. It was an innocuous enough statement, and yet it sounded as if she'd been feeling trapped.

"Do I make too many demands on your time?" His tone was dangerously cool. She knew he was only lashing out because he was still angry over the conversation with his mother.

"That's not what I meant. You've had so many meetings lately and it was nice to see my friend. That's all."

He shoved a hand through his hair and turned away. "I have work to do, Tina."

She walked over and stood behind him. She started to put a hand on his arm, but thought better of it. "Do you want to talk, Nico?"

He spun on her. "About what?" He jabbed a finger in the direction of the phone. "About my mother? There is nothing you can say, *cara*, that will change the situation."

Tina took a deep breath. "No, I didn't think I could. But you're obviously upset about it. Sometimes it helps to talk."

His laugh was harsh and bitter. "You know nothing of my life, Tina. Nothing. You can't just come in here and ask me to talk and think it will make everything better."

"I didn't say it would make it better. I said that sometimes it helps."

"You are a child," he spat at her. "A naive woman who knows nothing of relationships. You grew up sheltered by your family and loved no matter what. What would you know about a life like mine? My only value to my parents was that I was a boy and an heir."

His words stung her to the core, and yet she refused to walk away. She didn't know what it was like to be shuffled between parents, but she did understand what it was like to feel lonely. Though how could she compare her loneliness to his? She couldn't and she knew it.

"If it makes you feel better to heap scorn on me, then fine. Do it."

He stared at her for a long minute, his eyes flashing with pain. And then he swore as he took a step backward. "Just go, Tina. Leave me alone. I'll get over it soon enough."

Tina was sitting on the terrace with a cup of tea and her phone, texting Faith and pretending that everything was well. Faith sent pictures of Renzo and baby Domenico that caught at Tina's heart and made her ache with longing for what they had.

She didn't know if she and Nico would ever have that, but she could hope. Though it seemed a somewhat futile hope at the moment, she had to admit.

She felt guilty sending texts back and forth with no mention of her pregnancy and marriage, but it was clear that her brother didn't yet know. Thankfully. She couldn't imagine how angry he would be when he did, but she was certain it was going to be bad.

Faith had asked her to fly out and join them, but Tina refused, saying she and Lucia had plans to go to Tenerife. She felt bad telling a lie, but sending a text with the truth wasn't quite how she envisioned breaking the news to her family.

Finally, the texts ended and she sat and looked at the dome of St. Peter's in the distance. The bells sounded the hour while below the apartment she could hear the traffic whizzing by and the occasional shouts of people greeting or cursing each other in the street.

Rome was always bustling with activity. She loved the city, but right now she felt as if she would like to be somewhere quieter, more placid. Castello di Casari. She could still picture the beauty of that pergola—and the look in Nico's eyes when he'd got down on one knee to propose. It hadn't been real in the sense that they'd been in love, but he sure had made her believe for a second there.

"Tina."

She turned toward his voice. He stood in the terrace doors, watching her. His hands were in his pockets, his shoulder leaning against the door frame. He looked delicious, as always, and a tiny thrill flared to life in her belly. He was wearing a white shirt, unbuttoned to show a slice of skin, and a pair of faded jeans with loafers.

He walked over to her and stood beside her chair, not looking at her, but gazing out at the city lights. She wanted to twine her hand in his and press it to her cheek. *Love*, a voice whispered. *You love him.*

No, not love. Sympathy.

"Finish your work?" she asked brightly. She would not let him see how much he'd hurt her by shutting her out earlier.

He pulled a chair out and sat across from her. *"Sì."* He didn't say anything for a long minute. And then he pulled a small box from his pocket and set it on the table between them. When she didn't say anything, he pushed it toward her.

Her heart began to thrum. "What's this?" She took the velvet box, but she didn't open it.

"An apology," he said. "And something I neglected to do."

She popped the top open and stared. The diamond inside caught the light and refracted it, sparkling in the Roman dusk. It was at least six carats, she decided.

And it was surrounded by yet more diamonds. A very expensive and elegant ring.

"It's beautiful." It was true, and it made her heart ache. Perversely, she wanted it to mean something to him. But it didn't. He'd bought her a ring and now he was giving it to her along with an apology. As if the way to make up for not trusting her enough to talk to her was to buy her things.

Silly, silly Tina. But what had she expected?

He took the box from her and removed the ring. Then he slipped it onto her hand and she pulled it closer, turning her hand this way and that to catch the light.

"If you don't like it, you can pick something else."

She shook her head. The ring was gorgeous, and definitely something she would have chosen for herself. It wasn't modest or understated, but it wasn't gaudy, either. It was elegant, the kind of jewelry worn by a marchesa.

"Thank you," she said, keeping her eyes downcast so he wouldn't see the hint of sadness in them. He'd given her a wedding ring, but it didn't feel as if it meant anything to him. It was just one more thing to check off his list of things to do. And a way to soothe any hurt she might be feeling over the way he'd treated her earlier.

"I'm sorry I snapped at you," he said, as if on cue.

"You were upset."

"Nevertheless, it was not your fault."

"I shouldn't have said anything." She shrugged and played with her phone where it sat on the table. "Who am I to give advice? I'm pregnant and married and I still haven't told my family. Until I solve my problems, I probably shouldn't attempt to give advice on yours."

"Your family loves you, Tina. Renzo loves you. He's going to be angry, not because of what you've done, but because of who you've done it with. But he won't stop loving you."

It was her turn to be taken aback. "I'm sorry, but I don't see how you can possibly know that. He hates you, and I've betrayed him." She shook her head. "No, I don't think he'll stop loving me. But he won't want to see me."

He blew out a breath. "Why did you tell me about the baby? You didn't have to. If you hadn't, you wouldn't have to worry about what happens next."

The lump in her throat hurt, but she swallowed it down. "I can't believe you're asking me this when you wouldn't talk to me earlier." She spread her hands on the table, shaking her head. "But I'll tell you. I'll prove that you *can* talk about the things that bother you and the world won't end if you do. I told you about the baby because I grew up without a father. I always wanted to know who he was, but my mother wouldn't tell me. And I was determined that wouldn't happen to this child. I didn't expect you'd insist on getting married, however."

His eyes flashed. "No, you thought we'd live separate lives and I'd come visit the baby from time to time. When it was convenient, of course. And only so long as your brother didn't decide to prevent it."

She wanted to deny it, but the truth was that's exactly what she'd thought. She'd thought it would be so easy, that she would tell him she was pregnant, tell him she wanted nothing from him, and they'd arrange civilized visitation as the baby grew. She'd known Renzo wouldn't approve, but she'd intended to put her foot down.

She dropped her gaze from Nico's. "I won't deny it," she said. "I truthfully didn't think you'd be interested in being a father. I had hoped you would want to be a part of the baby's life, but I didn't expect it."

"I'd ask what gave you that idea, but I'm sure I can guess."

They both knew he'd been quite a fixture in the tabloids over the years. "You haven't exactly had any long-term relationships."

"In my experience, they don't work out."

A pinprick of pain throbbed in her heart. "Is that from personal experience or from observation? Because I'd say the two are not interchangeable."

He looked resigned for a moment. Uncertain. But then his expression hardened again. "My parents have rather warped my view of what a marriage is supposed to be."

"They are only two people," she said. "They don't represent everyone." She didn't even want to think about how his views impacted *their* marriage.

He shook his head. "Nevertheless, they are what I grew up with. They should have divorced years ago, but they stayed together instead and made each other miserable."

"And you," she added softly.

She expected he'd grow angry but he only ran his palms over his face before spearing her with a glare. "And me. Yes, they made me miserable. They still do."

"Why did you marry me, Nico?" She had to ask, in light of what he'd said about his parents' marriage.

He looked away, as if he couldn't quite face her at that moment. "You know why."

"Yes, I suppose I do. But what happens after the baby is born?"

He shrugged. "We take it a day at a time, Tina. I can promise you I won't ever let this child feel the way I felt.

And I'm confident you won't, either. We'll figure something out, and we'll be far better parents than I had."

Her heart thumped. He was actually talking to her, though she didn't know for how long. "I appreciate that. And I think I understand now."

"Understand what?"

She shrugged self-consciously. "You looked uncomfortable when Giuseppe expressed his sympathies for your father's death, and later, when I did, as if you didn't want them but felt you had to accept them anyway."

He didn't say anything for a long minute. He just stared at her, his nostrils flaring as if he were holding in a great deal of emotion. "The truth is that I despised him. But not always. I worshipped him for years, craved his affection—yes, even beyond my mother's. She's right about that. I did side with him when I grew older. She was so…bitchy and petty, while he seemed regal, controlled. But I soon realized he only cared about himself."

Tears sheened her eyes. She didn't care if he saw them. She reached for his hand, squeezed it tight. "I'm sorry, Nico."

He didn't jerk his hand from hers. Instead, he squeezed their palms together. "I wanted what you had," he said, the words almost choked from him. "I came to your place so often because I wanted to be a part of what your family had together. Your mother is kind, accepting. I loved sitting at the kitchen table with all of you and eating dinner. It felt far more real than anything else in my life at that time."

"I loved having you there," she admitted. "I think we all did. Renzo looked upon you like a brother."

He pulled his hand away then, and she regretted the

impulse to say such a thing. But it had been the truth. He and Renzo had been so close, and now they weren't.

And now he was closing up again. Closing in on himself like an exquisite flower that only bloomed for a few hours and then shut the world out once more.

"It was a long time ago," he said stiffly.

She swallowed the lump in her throat. "It could be that way again. If only you and Renzo would talk—"

"Maledizione," he swore, rocketing to his feet, his entire body vibrating with anger. She could only stare up at him in shocked fascination. "Don't you understand? I am a Gavretti. I ruin everything I touch."

He turned and stalked inside while she sat helplessly and stared at the suddenly shimmering dome of St. Peter's in the distance.

Not *everything*, she hoped.

CHAPTER ELEVEN

WHY had he told her those things? Nico paced inside the darkened study, angry with himself for letting her see that far into him. He hated being vulnerable. He'd sworn to himself, when he'd been eight years old and crying because his mother wouldn't let him come home on a school break, that he would never let anyone see how much he hurt ever again.

It was about survival. About appearing strong and self-sufficient. The world couldn't exploit what it didn't know. If he appeared strong, then he was strong.

Nico swore softly. He could see her through the window, sitting there on the terrace and not moving. The ring he'd given her sparkled in the lights, drawing his attention.

She sat so still. He wondered what she was thinking. He had an insane urge to go to her, to pull her into his arms and tell her—once more—that he was sorry. What was wrong with him? Why was he feeling soft when it came to her?

Dio, he'd already revealed things to her that he should not. He'd opened up a window into his soul when he'd told her how he felt about his parents.

And then, to compound his mistake, he'd admitted to her what her family had meant to him. How he'd been desperate to sit in their warm glow and just soak it up as if he belonged.

He'd been pitiful, like a starving dog staring into the back door of a restaurant, hoping for a few scraps to come his way. He, a Gavretti, the heir to an ancient title and estates around the world, had envied the humble home of the D'Angelis. He'd wanted to be one of them much more than he'd wanted to be Niccolo Gavretti.

But of course he hadn't belonged. It had taken almost two years, but he'd found that out the hard way. He'd told her he ruined everything he touched—and it was true. He and Renzo had been friends, working together on a project that meant everything to Renzo's future, and Nico had screwed it up.

He'd taken that feeling of belonging and thrown it back in their faces as if it had meant nothing. That's not at all what he'd intended when he'd gone to his father, but it's what had happened nevertheless. And he'd been powerless to stop it. Worse, he'd been complicit when he'd eventually done what his father had demanded of him.

She would hate him if she knew what he'd done. If she knew that he was directly responsible for Renzo's setback in the first year, that he had as good as reneged on his word, she would despise him. Even a baby wouldn't change that.

For the first time, he couldn't bear the thought of her knowing. Of her hating him. He'd forced her into this marriage with threats to her family because he'd believed marrying her was a shrewd move, as well as the right thing for the child, and he'd done it all without a care for how she felt about him.

Now he couldn't bear the idea she would hate him. God, what was wrong with him?

Nico stood with his fists clenched at his side and watched her through the window. Was she angry? Was she crying? He was on edge watching her. A sliver of desperation curled around his heart. He wanted to go outside and gather her in his arms, and then he wanted to take her to bed and pretend this had never happened. That he'd never spoken to her of his love-starved childhood and that he'd never let her know what her family had meant to him.

Because when she learned the truth, when she hated him and wanted out of this marriage, she would know how much he'd once cared about the D'Angelis. And she would pity him for it.

Dio, he was screwing this up in so many ways. He refused to have a marriage like his parents had had—a cold, bitter, soul-destroying relationship that had warped not only their lives but his as well—and yet he'd set himself up for it when he'd insisted on marrying the sister of the man he'd betrayed.

He wanted to go to her. He wanted to take her to bed and see her eyes darken with passion, wanted to hear her soft cries as he took them both over the edge of control, and then he wanted to lie beside her and go to sleep with her body tucked into the curve of his.

She fit there so perfectly. He loved resting his hand on her belly. It was far too early in the pregnancy to feel anything, but he liked knowing that his child nestled beneath his hand. He felt a connection there, something he'd never felt with another person, and he liked the way it made him feel inside.

Tina stood up then. Her beautiful body was outlined against the light, so lush and curvy that it made him ache just to look at her. Then she turned and came back inside. He held his breath for a long moment, hoping she would come into the office and challenge him, that she would put her arms around him and tell him she wanted him.

But she kept walking, down the hall and into the bedroom. He did not go after her.

"We're returning to Castello di Casari," Nico said, and Tina looked up from where she sat with her computer open on the couch. She'd been engaging in some light trading this morning, moving funds around and diversifying into a few tech stocks that she thought were poised for growth.

The financial papers were at her side, but she'd not read them yet. She usually liked to read them over breakfast, but she'd been too preoccupied. Even now, thoughts of last night warmed her cheeks and made her squirm in her seat.

Nico had come to bed late last night, slipping in beside her and lying on his back with an arm behind his head.

She'd pretended to be asleep, though she'd hoped he might reach for her anyway. He did not, so she'd turned toward him and put a hand on his chest. He still didn't reach for her, so she sidled closer and ran her palm down his flat abdomen.

He'd shuddered beneath her touch. And then he'd turned to her as if she'd flipped a switch inside him and tugged her into his arms.

"Tina," he'd groaned into her neck. "Tina."

She'd spread her hands on the hot, silky skin of his back. "Make love to me, Nico. Please. I want you so much."

What followed had been the most intense lovemaking between them yet. He'd worshipped her body reverently, as if he'd had forever to do so. As if they were suspended in time and the only thing that mattered was the two of them. He'd kissed his way down her torso, and then slid his tongue between her folds, swirling and sucking her clitoris until she came apart with a cry.

He did it again and again, until she'd begged him to join his body with hers and end the torture. He'd slid inside her, his body hard and strong, filling her so exquisitely. She'd thought she'd felt it all with him, but she'd realized in that moment she hadn't.

Because it felt different when you realized you really were in love with the man whose body knew yours so perfectly. But perhaps *different* was the wrong word. It felt like something...*more*.

More intense, more thrilling. More heartbreaking. Especially when the man you loved did not love you.

Tina gave herself a mental shake as she looked up at him now, her heart aching for him. How had she let it happen? How had she fallen in love with him between one breath and the next?

She'd thought she'd been on her guard, thought she'd been in control. She hadn't.

"I'd like that," she said in answer to his announcement. "I didn't get to explore it quite enough the last time."

Besides, there were shadows under his eyes and she worried that he'd been working too hard. It would be good to go somewhere more remote and peaceful. Somewhere that she wouldn't be worried about her brother showing up unannounced and having a meltdown.

"I've finished what I needed to do in Rome. We'll leave after lunch."

Tina was busy for the rest of the morning, packing

and getting ready to leave the city. She texted Lucia, who wished her a *buon viaggio* and told her to call every day, and then they were on their way.

This time when the helicopter swooped over the mountains and headed down to the imposing castle sitting in the lake, Tina paid attention to everything she had not before. The water was crystalline blue, turquoise in places, from the melt waters that came down out of the mountains and fed the lake.

Today, the sky was clear. Sailboats and motorboats dotted the lake. People sunned themselves on yachts, looking up with hands shading their eyes as the helicopter passed overhead.

"What a beautiful place," she said. "How they must envy you coming into the manor in the lake."

He laughed. "Perhaps they do. I've often thought we should open to tourists, but that was before I married you. Now I think we will keep the castle as our own private refuge from the world."

She liked the sound of that, though she felt slightly sorry for the tourists who would never get to visit. On the other hand, there were plenty of other tourist attractions nearby.

But even better, she liked that he'd said it would be *their* private refuge.

She turned her head to look out the window as the craft began its descent onto the helipad. The emotions whirling inside her were almost too much, and she was afraid that if he looked at her she would cry.

She desperately wanted to grab his hand, hold it to her cheek and tell him she loved him.

Instead, she swallowed the impulse and waved as she saw Giuseppe. He stood at the edge of the landing pad, his hair whipping in the breeze from the rotors even though he had very little of it. Behind him, several staff members waited, no doubt to help with the luggage.

Giuseppe waved back, and she smiled to herself, suddenly sure that it wasn't the most dignified thing in the world for him to do but that he'd done it for her.

"My lady," he said, bowing over her hand when they'd alighted from the helicopter and moved away from the rotors. "Congratulations on your marriage, and welcome once again to Castello di Casari. This time, you are her mistress and she is happy to have you."

"Thank you, Giuseppe," she said, smiling happily. Her world wasn't perfect, that was certain, but it had been a pretty good day thus far.

Nico put his arm around her and pulled her into the curve of his body. She wanted to turn into him, tuck her cheek against his chest and breathe him in.

Giuseppe grinned broadly as his gaze moved between them, and she knew that he'd seen what she couldn't hide.

"So happy to see a couple so deeply in love," he effused. "Maybe soon we can hope for the bambino, yes?"

She wasn't certain how Nico would react to that, but he only smiled and clapped Giuseppe on the shoulder. "Perhaps we can, Giuseppe. I'll see what I can do."

The other man laughed, and then they were going down the steps and into the castle the same way they'd gone before. This time, however, Nico took her up the stairs and into his room instead of the adjoining one she'd had the last time.

Once the door closed, he pulled her into his arms and kissed her at the same time he slipped the straps of her dress off her shoulders.

"What are you doing, Nico? They'll be bringing the

luggage up soon," she said, laughing as he dipped his lips to her shoulder.

"That's what locks are for, *cara*. Besides, I did promise Giuseppe I'd get started on the baby making."

"I think it's safe to say that task is done," she replied. His fingers went to her zipper and started sliding it down slowly.

"Just to be certain, I think we should get naked anyway." He reached behind him and flipped the lock on the door, then picked her up and carried her to the bed. He quickly divested her of her clothes, though he still wore all of his as he hovered over her on his palms. It was rather erotic to feel the scrape of his jeans against her sensitized skin.

"Wait," she cried as a thought occurred to her.

He looked up, his beautiful stormy-gray eyes hot and intense. "What, *cara*? Do you have a request?"

Now, there was a thought. "No," she said quickly. "But your father—it, um, it wasn't this bed, right?"

Nico laughed. "Definitely not. He was in Florence at the time. Besides, I have ordered new mattresses for all the residences."

"I'm relieved to hear it."

He bent and licked her nipple, and a shot of liquid desire melted in her core. "Now, about that request," he murmured. "Tell me what you desire from me, Tina… anything you desire."

The next few days were glorious. Tina had never been happier. She felt so free, as if she really could be whomever she wanted. As if she truly were bold and brave, and not a cowering mouse deep inside. Nico made her feel that way—as if she could conquer the world and not regret a single moment of it.

Each day, they started with breakfast on the terrace where they laughed and talked and teased each other with hot looks and silly innuendo.

They sometimes went for walks around the garden, or took a swim in the warm pool. Once, they went out in a yacht and floated along the lake's shore, stopping at one of the towns for lunch and some shopping.

Every night, they stayed up late, making love, watching television, or sitting side by side in the bed and working on their computers. It was domestic and blissful and she looked forward to the days stretching before her so long as they began and ended with Nico.

Today, they'd been swimming when he'd suddenly given her one of those heated looks that she knew preceded an afternoon of hot lovemaking. She hadn't even pretended not to notice. Instead, she'd climbed out of the pool and toweled off while he'd watched her.

And then she'd told him she'd race him to the bed. She could hear him lifting out of the water behind her as she'd started to run, laughing, but he'd never managed to catch her. She'd made it to the bedroom first, and when he arrived, he'd still had water dripping down his hard, tanned muscles.

He hadn't even dried off before stripping her bikini and coming down on top of her.

After they made love, she fell into a sound sleep, waking sometime late in the afternoon, her body replete, her skin still glowing and sensitive. She turned toward Nico, but he wasn't in bed. She frowned as she sat up, yawning and stretching.

She had to stop sleeping in the middle of the day. And she had to tell him to stop letting her do so.

Except that she knew he wouldn't listen. He'd nod and say of course—but if she slept, he would let her sleep. Apparently, according to him, the pregnancy website said excessive tiredness was common in the first trimester. Nico was turning into quite the authority on pregnancy, she thought wryly.

Her phone buzzed with a text. Occasionally, she got enough of a signal to get a message or two, usually when the sky was clear. Tina reached for her phone, pleased that someone was getting through. There were three bars today, which were a good sign, and a text from Faith.

What's going on there? Is everything okay?

Tina swallowed a sliver of dread and texted back. Of course. Everything is fine.

A second later, her phone buzzed again. Renzo is worried about you.

I'm fine.

There was something in the paper about you being seen with Niccolo Gavretti in Rome a few days ago.

Tina's heart sank. She'd been expecting something to happen, knowing the way the tabloids usually covered Nico, but she'd allowed herself to be lulled into a false sense of security when nothing had happened. At least they didn't have the story of her hasty marriage yet.

Nico and I move in the same circles sometimes. It wouldn't be unusual to see him at an event. Oh, the irony of lying about seeing Nico while sitting in his bed.

The pause before the next text was long. Finally, her phone buzzed. He's dangerous, Tina. He wouldn't think twice about using you in order to get to Renzo. Be careful.

Tina's heart twisted. She wanted to call Faith up and tell her how wrong she was, but it would do no good. Faith had her information from Renzo, and of course she would take her husband's side.

Tina sighed. What a mess she'd gotten herself into. She loved the man her brother hated, and she still had no idea what had happened between them. Clearly, her reprieve was nearly up and she had to tell Renzo the truth before the papers said anything more. But she wasn't going to do it through a text to his wife.

I will.

Faith texted a few more things, a picture of baby Domenico sleeping in his crib, and they said their good-byes. Tina got up and dressed, and then took the newspapers she'd not read this morning and went out onto the terrace. The afternoon sun was less intense, and the shade of the laurels kept her cool while she flipped through the papers.

They were financial papers, not tabloids, but she still scanned them for any news about Nico that might appear.

When she found it, her chest felt tight.

Gavretti Manufacturing Cash Flow Shortage, Order Cancellations.

She read the article twice to be sure she understood everything the reporter speculated. Then she got up and went to find Nico. They'd been here for days, and he'd said nothing. It bothered her and worried her at the same time.

She found him where she expected, in his home office with its gorgeous paneled walls, floor-to-ceiling bookcases and overstuffed leather furniture. He sat at the desk and tapped on his computer. Three phones lay on the desk in front of him.

Nico looked up as she walked in, the frown he'd worn easing when their gazes locked.

She ignored the jolt of electricity buzzing through her system and held up the paper. "Is this true?"

The warmth in his eyes faded to something akin to resignation. "Not all of it."

"Which part is true then?"

She thought he wouldn't tell her, but he sighed and leaned back in the chair. "My father left me a mess. I'm trying to fix it."

"By raiding your company?"

"By shifting assets temporarily."

She came over and sat down in front of his desk. "I want to help."

He shook his head. "I have it under control. I have advisers and a crack financial team. We're handling it."

Worry spiked in her belly. "You're vulnerable right now."

His eyes flashed. They both knew what she did not say. "Somewhat, yes. But trying to take me over would strain D'Angeli Motors. It would not be the wisest of courses that Renzo could take."

"And yet whatever this thing is between you doesn't seem to care about logic." Tina shook her head and swore. "So stubborn, the both of you!"

She hadn't brought up the subject in days, and he'd not, either. Now, he looked irritated.

"It's complicated, Tina."

She smacked her hand on the desk, startling him if the way he flinched was any indication. "It's not complicated at all. You talk, you solve what needs to be solved, and you walk away with a clear conscience.

No one says you have to be best friends again, but for God's sake, there is a child on the way and he or she will need a whole family, not half of one."

"The baby will have the two of us," he grated. "That is enough."

She shook her head furiously. "There is also an aunt and uncle and cousin, as well as a grandmother, who would all spoil this child rotten if given the chance."

His jaw flexed stubbornly. "I won't stop you from seeing them, Tina."

She could feel angry tears welling behind her eyelids. "No, but you won't join me, either. You'll force me to choose between spending time with you and spending time with them, provided Renzo will see me at all after he finds out I've married you." A bubble of hysterical laughter escaped her throat. "My God, it's like you and my brother got a divorce and I'm being torn between you."

"Don't be melodramatic," he snapped. "You aren't a child."

"No, I'm not," she said fiercely. "But I still lo—care about you both."

She couldn't say *love*, though she wanted to. She couldn't bear for him to look at her with pity when he knew how she felt. By now, she knew enough about him to know that love was not something that would ever come easy for him. He would always be suspicious, always mistrusting. He'd been hurt too badly by the lack of love in his life to believe it could be so freely given or genuine.

Tina leaned forward, palms on the desk, determination vibrating in every bone of her body. "Let me help, Nico. I know what I'm doing, and I can help you get the company back in the black. Renzo won't be able to touch it. I'll make sure of it."

He looked stunned. And then angry. "By doing what? Begging him not to?"

"I wasn't going to beg him, no." Though she had intended to have Faith put pressure on Renzo in the interim, she also intended to inject enough cash into the coffers to make the prospect unappealing to him.

Nico shot to his feet and swore. "Do you honestly believe I'd trust you, Tina? We've been married for less than a month. We have a child on the way, and we have great sex—but you've been a D'Angeli your entire life. Your loyalty is to your family, not to me."

She felt as if he'd slapped her. But what had she expected? Of course he was suspicious, and why not? She would be, too, if she were him. She stood and folded her arms beneath her breasts, feeling angry and drained and frustrated all at once.

Her loyalty *was* to her family—but he was her family, too. That was the part he hadn't managed to get through his thick skull yet. She loved him, and Renzo didn't *need* Gavretti Manufacturing. Oh, she didn't doubt he would do everything in his power to obtain it if he could, but the fact was that D'Angeli Motors was thriving and growing, and her brother was in no danger of losing a thing.

Nico, on the other hand, was dancing on the edge of a precipice and too infuriatingly stubborn to see that he needed her.

"I know why you think that, Nico. It hurts to hear you say it, but I understand why you would." She crumpled the newspaper and tossed it on the desk. "And don't think I don't realize, in light of this news, that at least part of why you married me was to buy leverage against Renzo."

He didn't deny it, and though her heart throbbed, she told herself it didn't matter. She knew enough about him now to understand that he didn't trust anyone. He might have been from a privileged background, but he'd been so lonely that he'd learned to do whatever it took to protect himself.

"It wasn't my only reason," he said stiffly.

She shook her head. "No, I realize that. Now what you need to realize is that I may be what you need to get out of this mess, though not in the way you imagined." She reached for a pen and wrote some figures down on the notepad sitting beside his computer. "This is what I've done with my money. Tell me you could have done better and I won't say another word."

CHAPTER TWELVE

"What's your plan?"

Tina looked up to find him standing in the entrance to the pergola, watching her. She'd been reading—or trying to read, since she was in fact fuming and unable to concentrate. She'd fled his office and then fled the house, angry and sad and in need of some distance. Since there wasn't really anywhere to go, she'd opted for the shaded pergola.

Now, she set the eReader on the table in front of her and searched his eyes. He looked serious, though unhappy. He didn't want to ask her this, she knew. And yet the numbers on the paper didn't lie. She *did* have a good head for finance.

"You need cash," she said, deciding not to dance around the obvious. "I have cash. We'll cover the loan payments to buy time to restructure the debt. And then, if you'll let me see the complete picture, I'll have a better idea what else can be done."

He didn't even blink when she mentioned loan payments. But she'd done her research and she had a far better idea of what he was trying to do now. The state of his father's finances at the time of his death was a matter of record. Anyone determined to do so could find out the information.

In trying to save the ancient estate from ruin, Nico was putting his company at risk.

"And what makes you think my financial advisors haven't already suggested this course of action?"

"Oh, I'm sure they did. But the cash is clearly coming out of Gavretti Manufacturing. You may not be damaging the company, but you're putting your entire personal stake at risk. Someone could buy your loans and take the company out from under you. You're right that it wouldn't be easy just yet—but that day is probably coming, and sooner than you wish."

He looked at her for a long minute. And then he shook his head. "Your brother is indeed a fool not to use you."

She shrugged self-consciously. "I'm not a genius. I'm just good with figuring these kinds of things out."

He pulled the paper she'd written the numbers on from his pocket. "I don't know. I'd say this is impressive. No wonder you were so insistent about your money in Gibraltar."

She laced her fingers together in her lap. "It's what I enjoy doing. I have fun with numbers—and with taking chances on them."

"You're good at it, apparently."

"I think I am," she said.

He set the paper on the table. "Nevertheless, I don't need your money, Tina. Your analysis is interesting—and even, I admit, tempting—but I already have a plan."

Disappointment ate at her. Stubborn man. He didn't want her money because of who she was. "You still don't trust me."

He blew out a breath. "I shouldn't have said that."

"But it's what you feel."

His eyes gleamed hot. "Haven't you figured it out by now? I don't trust anyone."

Her heart hurt for him because she knew there was so much more underlying that statement than he would admit to. He didn't trust anyone because he'd never been able to depend on anyone. He was used to doing everything alone, to taking care of himself and asking nothing of those from whom he should be able to ask the world.

In that moment, she despised his parents more than she'd ever despised anyone in her life. Her fingers clenched. If she could get her hands around his mother's neck right now...

Not helpful.

Tina swallowed, her throat aching with the weight of unshed tears. "You need to learn how, Nico. Not everyone is your enemy."

He looked remote and cool and untouchable, and it hurt to see him withdraw from her after all they'd shared. "I learned a long time ago that it was easier to live life as if they were. It keeps me from being disappointed."

"I'm not everyone," she said. "I care."

"Yes, but for how long?" He took a step closer, his hands thrust in his pockets, his eyes glittering bright as diamonds. "Everyone has a limit, Tina. Even you. You haven't asked me in days now what happened between Renzo and me. Why not? Are you afraid the truth might change your mind?"

He watched her struggle and knew he'd said something that pierced to the very heart of her. Yes, she said she cared—but if she knew the truth, what then? Would she believe him guilty, or would she still try to see the best in him?

He very much feared it would be the first option. And that's what bothered him—the fact he actually *cared* what she thought. Why?

He'd initially decided to marry her for the child—and for leverage, yes—and to hell with the consequences. He didn't care what she thought of him, so long as she was a good mother to their baby.

But somewhere along the way, that had changed. He craved her like a drug. He didn't like it. Or he did like it when he was deep inside her and making her scream his name, but he didn't like the way it made him feel out of control to want her so much.

It was almost as if he *needed* her somehow. And that was not true, because he didn't need anyone. He'd made sure of it.

"I'm not afraid," she said. "I stopped asking because it makes you angry."

What made her different from other women? She was smart and beautiful, but so what? She challenged him in unexpected ways, which should irritate him and yet somehow managed to thrill him. He didn't quite know what it was, but it was something.

He'd sat in his office after she'd left and stared at the figures on the paper as though they were written in Sanskrit. And, *Dio*, he'd been tempted. Tempted to accept her money and let her forge this path by his side. It would certainly make what he was trying to do easier.

But then he'd wondered just what in the hell he was thinking. She was still a D'Angeli, regardless of their marriage, and she would inevitably side with her brother against him. It didn't matter that she craved him in bed, or that she was pregnant with his child. Blood was thicker than water.

Hell, in his world, even blood wasn't enough to ensure unwavering loyalty. How could he expect it from her?

No, he wouldn't take her money, no matter how tempting.

"Are you planning to tell me now," she asked, one delicate eyebrow arching imperiously. "Or was that simply a cryptic teaser designed to put me off?"

"It's simple enough," he said, his heart pounding much more quickly than it should now that he'd determined to tell her everything. Once he told her, she would despise him—and then he could go back to living the way he always did, the way he understood. He would still have her in his bed and in his life, but neither of them would mistake what they had for anything other than sexual chemistry and a shared future for the sake of their child.

"Renzo and I worked on the design for the prototype for months. I promised to get the financial backing for us to make a test version of the motorcycle."

She nodded. "I remember how excited he was. It was all either of you talked about."

He remembered those days as if they'd happened only yesterday. The memory of them still had the power to slice into him with pain and regret. He should have been stronger.

"Yes, well, I failed. And not only that, I betrayed him in the process. Gavretti Manufacturing was up and running a full year before D'Angeli Motors."

She sat there with her jaw slightly open and her eyes wide. So she had not known that fact.

"That's right," he said, pressing in for the kill, though

it destroyed him inside to watch the expression on her face. "I stole the prototype. I made the motorcycle without Renzo. That's why he hates me. And that's why you shouldn't want to give me your money."

"I don't believe it," she said after a long minute in which he could hear everything around him as if it were magnified a thousandfold. The chirping of birds, the beat of a butterfly's wings, the sticky slide of a spider in its web.

He refused to allow that tiny leap of his heart to give him hope. "Why not, *cara*? You already know I don't trust anyone. Why wouldn't I take the plans and start my own company?"

Her hands clenched into fists. "You might be bad, Nico—or you've made everyone think you're bad—but that's not who you are. You wouldn't steal the prototype when you'd spent months working on it together. When you knew what it meant to Renzo."

"How can you be so sure?"

"Because it's not who you are," she repeated.

"You don't know that. It might be exactly who I am."

She shot to her feet with a growl and glared at him. "It's *not*, so stop trying to make me think it is."

Something broke inside him then, something he hadn't even known was there. The force of it was too much, whipping him in a maelstrom of emotion while he stood there and focused on her beautiful, angry face, unable to say even a word.

How could she look at him like that and believe, to her core, that he had not done what everyone else thought he'd done? No one had ever believed in him that strongly. No one had ever stood toe to toe with him and insisted he wasn't what he said he was. When he'd felt petty and mean and unloved, no one had ever told him differently.

When he'd been ruthless and hard and colder than New Year's Day at the North Pole to survive, no one had ever told him they didn't believe that's who he was.

But she was standing here now, this woman he adored, and telling him he was so much better than he thought.

This woman he adored.

Dio!

Panic followed hard on the heels of that revelation. How could he adore her when she would leave him in the end?

Nico took a step backward. He didn't adore her. He *wanted* her. He was confusing the two in his head, that's all.

She looked miserable. A tear spilled free and slid down her cheek and his heart turned inside out. He wanted to gather her to him and hold her tight, tell her everything. But he couldn't. He couldn't be that weak ever again.

Nico turned and walked away.

Tina despised crying. But she'd been doing a lot of it over the past few hours. First, she'd watched in stunned silence as Nico had left her in the garden. She'd been torn between chasing after him and making him talk to her, or staying where she was until she got herself under control again. She'd been so angry and so hurt at the same time.

And, yes, even confused. He'd told her that he'd stolen the plans from Renzo—but she didn't believe him. She simply didn't, and yet she was furious with him for not telling her the rest of the story. For turning and walking away like a coward.

As if he *wanted* her to believe the worst.

She didn't know how much time passed—a half an hour at most maybe—when she'd heard the helicopter coming in for a landing. Fear had slid through her like oil then. She'd shot to her feet and started running toward the castle.

But she was too late. By the time she bounded up the stairs to the helipad, the craft had lifted off and started banking toward the mountains. She knew without being told that Nico was on it. She'd stood there with her hands twisting together in front of her and felt empty inside.

He'd left her. He'd climbed onto that damn helicopter and left her.

She went to her bedroom—their bedroom—and raged for a good hour. Then she'd cried for another. And then she'd picked up her phone and tried to text Lucia. But the signal was intermittent and she couldn't get it to go.

Giuseppe brought her dinner on a tray. He looked confused, and apologetic. "It was business, madam," he said, as if that explained everything. "His lordship will return in a day or two. I'm sure it must have been important for him to leave you on your honeymoon."

"Thank you, Giuseppe," Tina said numbly. Yes, business. Important business. Perhaps he was even now prowling the nightclubs of Rome and finding a woman to spend the night with.

The thought made her heart hurt so badly she thought she might throw up. *No*, she told herself fiercely. *He would not do that.*

Just as he wouldn't have stolen the prototype. How

could the man who spent hours on pregnancy websites, who flew dresses in for their wedding, and who sat with his head in his hands and fought the specter of his unfeeling mother *not* have a heart? He'd told her how much he'd loved her family, and knowing what she did about his past, she didn't believe he'd lied about that.

He *did* have a heart. He was a man who felt things deeply, no matter that he tried to hide that fact from everyone, including himself. He was afraid of feeling. Afraid of loving.

And so was she, apparently. Tina frowned. Why hadn't she told him that she loved him? That she believed in him because she knew it in her bones that he was worthy of that belief?

Coward. She was no better than he was. He'd run from her, but she'd been running from the moment he'd walked into her hotel room in Rome. How could they possibly have a future together if they both kept running?

Tina lifted her chin as sudden determination rushed through her. She was finished running. No, from now on she was facing life head-on and demanding only the best it had to give. No more half measures for her. And no more hiding.

Determined, she flipped open her computer and started writing the emails that would change everything.

She gave him three days. When Nico still hadn't returned after that time, Tina dredged up every shred of haughty at her disposal and told Giuseppe she wanted the helicopter. She'd thought he might argue with her, or that Nico had given him orders to keep her on the island, but he merely nodded his head vigorously and said, "Yes, madam. Of course, madam."

She felt bad for being so brusque after that, but she'd been afraid he would refuse her. When she stood inside the glassed-in waiting room and watched for the helicopter on the horizon, she turned to him and smiled.

"I'm sorry if I was rude earlier, Giuseppe."

He dipped his head. "Not at all, madam. You miss his lordship. It is quite understandable."

The helicopter soon arrived to whisk Tina back to the airport and then to Rome. She didn't know for certain that's where he was, but she suspected it since there was so much going on with Gavretti Manufacturing. Once she landed, she took a car to the apartment. Nico wasn't there, but the doorman recognized her and let her in when she claimed she'd forgotten her key.

That was another item on her list of things to do: get keys to all Gavretti residences. Nico wasn't hiding from her ever again.

She went down the hall to the bedroom, discovered that he was indeed staying there, and then turned and went back to the living area where she made a couple of phone calls before settling down to wait.

She didn't even have to wait an hour. The door burst open and he was there, looking so delicious in his navy blue custom suit with the pin-striped shirt open at the neck.

He also looked furious. Obviously, the concierge had done as she asked and called Nico to let him know she had arrived.

"What are you doing here, Tina? And why didn't you let me know you were coming? You should have had security."

She stood and faced him squarely across the couch.

Her heart swelled with love for him. He looked so angry, but she only wanted to touch him. She wanted to put her palms on his face and tell him how much she loved him.

But she was too scared. She would do it, but not quite yet.

"You didn't steal the prototype, Nico," she said, ignoring his questions. "I want you to tell me the truth."

He swore violently. She expected him to fight her, but he went over and poured a Scotch from the liquor cabinet before turning back to her.

"I might as well have. It was my fault."

"How?"

He sank onto a chair across from her and rubbed his forehead. And then his gaze snapped up, glaring at her.

"I took a copy of the plan to my father, to ask him for the money. He refused. He told me he would only back us if I built the motorcycles and made it a family enterprise." He took a sip of the Scotch. "I told him no. But he had friends who followed the sport, and he took the design to them, looking for investors. The next thing I knew, the financing was in place for Gavretti Manufacturing. Renzo didn't believe me. We said terrible things to each other—and I went to work for my father."

"I thought it was your company?"

"I bought it from him a few years later, but no, it was not at first."

Tina blinked. "But he didn't care about motorcycles, did he? Why would he try to start a factory that built them?"

Nico took another swallow of the Scotch. "Greed. He saw something in the plan and wanted to capitalize on it. He was right, as the success of the company proves."

Tina clenched her fingers in her lap. "You have to tell Renzo this."

His eyes flashed, his jaw hardening. "I did tell him, Tina. He didn't believe me." He laughed harshly. "Can you blame him? In his eyes, I betrayed him because I believed I was better than he was. Because I was a rich and privileged Gavretti."

She couldn't stop the feelings swelling in her another minute. He was a good man, and he tortured himself so much. Not only that, but he expected people to believe the worst of him.

She went to his side, knelt on the floor before him, and grasped his free hand in hers.

"No," he told her, setting the Scotch down and trying to make her get up. "Don't get on the floor."

"Nico," she said, tears rushing into her throat and eyes. "I believe you. *I* believe you."

He pulled her up and into his lap, and she clung to him, buried her face against his neck and breathed him in. He was everything to her, everything. Him, the baby. She couldn't imagine her life without them now. And she was more than prepared to do battle with her brother over it.

"You're too trusting, Tina," he said, stroking her hair. "I *did* go to work for my father. A better man would have refused."

"And let him steal all the hard work you and Renzo did? I don't think so."

"I asked Renzo to come work for me. I thought we could still do what we wanted—but he refused. And he was right to do so, as the success of D'Angeli Motors proves."

She pressed her palm against his chest, felt how fast

his heart was beating. "You were both so stubborn. And wrong to let this fester between you."

"It can't be fixed, Tina," he told her. "There's too much bad blood between us now. We've spent too many years feeling bitter and angry. I know I've said things, done things, that can't be forgiven."

She squeezed him tight. "We'll see about that."

The door buzzed then, and she took a deep breath to fortify herself for what came next. It wasn't going to be an easy afternoon.

She just hoped the two men she loved most didn't hate her by the end of it.

CHAPTER THIRTEEN

HER brother was so furious he vibrated with it. Beside him, Faith had a hand on his arm. She squeezed it at regular intervals, as if to remind him he couldn't do what he so obviously wanted to do, which was to punch Nico.

Faith shot Tina a worried look, and Tina clenched her jaw. She'd done this, and now she had to see it through. Worse, she'd dragged Faith into it when she'd asked her to help set up the meeting. Renzo would not be happy about that, either. Right now, he was too focused on her and Nico to be angry at Faith.

"This is a low blow even for you, Nico," Renzo snarled. "You couldn't touch me, so you went after my sister?"

"Renzo," Tina snapped, and he slanted his icy gaze at her. "Didn't you read the email I sent you? We met at a masquerade. We didn't know each other's identity."

"That's what he wants you to think."

Tina rolled her eyes. My God, he sounded like Nico had in the hotel room when he'd accused her of setting him up. "The two of you are exactly alike. It's no wonder you won't talk."

Nico was standing over by the liquor cabinet again. He hadn't refilled his glass, but he stood there with his hands in his pockets, his gaze flashing furiously at her and Renzo both. He looked like a cornered animal. And a dangerous one.

"There's nothing to talk about, Tina," Nico growled. "You see how he thinks."

Tina resisted the urge to pinch the bridge of her nose. Instead, she went over to her brother and touched his arm, even though he was so very angry with her.

"Renzo, for God's sake, there's a baby on the way. Nico is my husband now. You *both* made mistakes, you know. And I want you to talk to each other about them."

Renzo's expression was thunderous. "You can't be serious, Tina. He cares nothing for you. This is all a game to him."

"I *am* serious." So serious that her chest hurt with the chaotic emotions buffeting her. It was an effort not to cry. Her eyes stung, her throat ached and her heart tattooed the inside of her chest at light speed. She loved them both, and they were idiots. "It's not a game."

Renzo swore. "You're a fool, you know that?"

She lifted her chin and stared at him with all the imperiousness she could manage. It hurt to hear him say that but, strangely, she wasn't feeling cowed. She'd always wanted her brother's approval—but now, for what must be the first time in her life, she realized she didn't need it.

"I'm twenty-four years old, Renzo. Old enough to make my own decisions. I don't need you deciding what's best for me anymore. I'm married to Nico and pregnant with his child—and that's not going to change."

He looked fierce. And so worried for her that it broke her heart.

"Tina, for God's sake, he betrayed me. Betrayed *us*. I almost didn't get the financing for the company after that. If I had not, you'd probably be waiting tables in some restaurant and trying to make ends meet. Our lives would *not* be what they are today. He tried to take that from us, *cara mia*."

She leaned toward him then, feeling fiercer than she'd ever felt in her life. "If you believe that, *you're* the fool."

"Renzo," Faith said in that syrupy Southern drawl of hers. "Why don't the two of you talk, for Tina's sake? You can at least be civil for her, can't you?"

Tina had the feeling that if anyone else had said that, including her, he'd have snapped their head off. Instead, he closed his eyes and squeezed his wife's hand, as if seeking patience and strength.

"Fine, yes. We will talk."

Tina went over to Nico, her heart in her throat. He was every bit as murderously angry as her brother, and she wasn't sure he would agree. She took his hand, and when he didn't stop her, she felt hopeful.

"I want you to do this for me, Nico. For our baby. Please."

His eyes flashed. And then he squeezed her hand and she drew in a shaky breath. "For you," he said. Then he lifted his head and glared at Renzo. "We can talk on the terrazzo."

"No," Tina said. "Faith and I will go outside. You two stay in here."

His brows drew together in concern. "It's hot out there, *tesoro*."

"We'll sit beneath the umbrella. Besides, I'm fairly positive neither of us will try to throw the other one off the roof. I'm not so sure about the two of you."

* * *

When the door to the terrazzo closed, Nico turned to look at the man glaring at him so murderously. They'd been best friends once, almost like brothers, but they'd been enemies for so many years now that he remembered that time as if it had happened to someone else.

"Drink?" he said.

Renzo shook his head. Nico refilled his own and leaned against the bar. He waited for it to happen, waited for the storm brewing inside Renzo to break. The man might have promised his sister to talk, but that hadn't changed his view in the least.

"I can't believe you went after Tina," Renzo said, his voice low and hard. "She had nothing to do with what happened between us."

"No," Nico drawled, "she didn't."

"Yet it didn't stop you."

Suddenly, Nico was tired of this charade. He turned to glance out the window at Tina, who sat beneath the umbrella with her sister-in-law and cast worried glances toward the door. She was beautiful, fierce and lovely. Special.

She believed in him, and nothing he said or did had shaken that belief. He'd been expecting her to leave, to hate him, but she didn't. No, she followed him and confronted him and demanded he face his past head-on in order to free his future.

And he wanted to do it. For her, he would do anything.

Anything to see her smile, to have her in his bed beside him, soft and warm and sexy. He wanted her there, on her computer, making her stock trades and giving him hell. And he wanted to watch her grow big with their baby, knowing she loved this child so fiercely that she'd come to him in the first place so that her baby would have a father.

Their baby.

The feeling that had gripped him in the garden the other day seized him again. Only this time it wouldn't let go until he acknowledged it for what it was.

Love. He loved her, and it stunned him. He'd never loved anyone—or hadn't since he'd been a child and learned that loving your parents didn't mean they had to love you back.

He wanted to go to her, wanted to sweep her into his arms and tell her how he felt. She'd fought for him so hard, fought against him, too, when he'd tried to keep her at arm's length. She'd crawled beneath his defenses and curled up in his heart.

Nico turned back to face Renzo, his chest swelling with emotion. He didn't really care what this man thought of him—but he did care what Tina thought. And Tina loved her brother. He hoped like hell she loved him, too. Because he wasn't ever letting her go.

"I love her, Renzo." The words felt so foreign coming out of his mouth. So new. "I don't care if you believe that or not, but it's the truth. And I will do anything to make her happy. If that means talking to you, then I'll do it for as long as she wants me to."

Renzo looked taken aback. But then his eyes narrowed. "Why should I believe a word of what you say?"

Nico took a deep breath. "I don't care if you believe it. Whether or not you do doesn't change the truth of how I feel."

Renzo snorted. "My God, you're unbelievable. Somehow, you've got her believing the lies you spout. And don't think I don't know you're doing this to protect your company. I've heard whispers of your trouble.

You think the only reason I won't destroy you is because of my sister. Don't bet on it, Nico."

"You once said to me that the motorcycles weren't my passion as they were yours. You were right." He shrugged. "I enjoy what I do, but it's not my life. If you want to take it away from me to prove a point, then do it."

"You're bluffing."

Nico shook his head. "No. Not only that, but I'll also tell you exactly how to truly destroy me, if that's what you wish." He turned to look at Tina again, felt his heart swelling with feeling. "Take her away from me, Renzo. That's how to do it."

Renzo didn't say anything for a long moment. "If you're lying to me about this—" He broke off, swore.

"I don't want to fight with you anymore. I should have never gone to work for my father. I should have found another way. I should have blown up the plant before allowing the first motorcycle to come off the line, but I didn't. I've made mistakes. I regret them. But I won't let them harm the woman I love any longer."

Renzo looked fierce. "If you hurt her, I'll make you wish you were never born."

"If anything ever happens to Tina, you won't have to."

They didn't seem to talk for as long as she'd hoped, but they had at least spent twenty minutes together without either of them throwing a punch. Faith gave Tina a hug and said she'd call soon, and Renzo stood in the door looking more thoughtful than he had when he'd walked in earlier.

"*Ciao*, Tina," he said softly. And then he opened his arms and she went into them, relieved and shaken and so very grateful that he wasn't going to shut her out. He kissed her on the head. "If he makes you happy, then I am content."

"I'm sorry for causing you pain, Renzo. But I love you. And I love Nico, too."

Renzo squeezed her before setting her away from him. "We will see you soon, I hope? Domenico has grown. You will be very surprised when you see him."

Tina wiped her eyes as she laughed. "I look forward to it."

Renzo and Faith left then, and Tina turned around to look at Nico. But he wasn't standing by the terrace door any longer. He was outside, standing in the middle of the terrace, lost in thought.

She went out to him, her heart thrumming. She didn't doubt he was angry with her, but she hoped that, like Renzo, he would forgive her. She didn't think he and Renzo had solved their problems, but she hoped they might have at least managed a truce. One day, maybe, forgiveness would come for them both. But for now, she'd settle for them being together and not looking like two wolves circling for the kill.

The sun had dropped lower in the sky, and the shadows lengthened across the terrazzo. Across the way, she could see an old woman hanging washing on her balcony.

Nico turned, as if he could feel her approach. What she saw in his eyes made her heart skip a beat.

"I'm sorry, Tina," he said before she could say a word.

"For what? I'm the one who forced you to spend time with my brother."

He took a deep breath. "For leaving you. For doubting that you could believe in me. For everything."

"Hopefully not everything," she said lightly, trying to keep from throwing herself into his arms and begging him to love her the way she loved him.

Love would come in time, she was certain. She could be patient. She *would* be patient.

She took a deep breath. "I'd be grieved, for instance, if you said you were sorry for the way you can't keep your hands off me. Or if you said you were sorry you'd married me."

He shook his head. "I'm not sorry for that."

Then he reached out and tugged her into his arms, and relief melted through her.

"I'm not sorry for it, either." She sighed and pressed her cheek to his chest. "I'm going to prove to you that this can work between us."

He lifted a hand and pushed her hair from her face. "I already believe it."

She tilted her head back to look up at him, her entire body tensing with hope. "You do?"

His smile lit her world. "I love you, Tina. And I believe there's nothing you can't do when you set your mind to it."

Tina felt her jaw drop. "You love me? Really?"

"I do."

"Oh, Nico, I love you, too," she said, tears filling her eyes. Good heavens, these hormones were making her weepy.

"I know you do."

"But I've never said it. How did you know?"

He laughed, the sound breaking as if he, too, were feeling overwhelmed with emotion. "You stood up to your brother and told him you believed me. I think you even called him a fool." He kissed the tip of her nose. "I truly enjoyed that, by the way. But you've also defended me fiercely and never once backed down, not even when I tried to make you do so."

"Of course I did. I love you."

"Yes, that's what I thought. You'd either have to love me or be insane. I chose the option I most wanted."

She curled her fists into his shirt. "I used to want this when I was a girl, you know. You, me, marriage. But I didn't really know what any of that meant. I just knew that you were perfect and I wanted you to love me."

He shook his head. "I've never been perfect. But I'm going to try every day of my life to be the best man I can be. For you and our children."

Tina laughed, though a tear escaped and rolled down her cheek. "You already are the best man you can be, Nico. You always have been. And your best is pretty damn good."

He dipped his head and kissed her fiercely. "I want to shout it to the rooftops how much I love you. In fact...*I love Valentina D'Angeli Gavretti!*"

Across the way, the woman hanging laundry stopped. *"Brava, amore,"* she shouted back.

Others took up the cry until Tina was laughing and crying and trying to hide behind Nico. He took her hand and dragged her inside.

"I love you," he told her, his mouth against her skin, his fingers divesting her of her clothing. "I love you..."

Tina never doubted him for a moment.

EPILOGUE

TINA looked up from the computer screen when Nico walked in, holding their son in his arms. The baby's little head lolled against his father's chest as he fought sleep, and Tina's heart squeezed hard with love for her men.

"What are you working on?" he asked.

"The latest projections. I believe you're going to turn a profit, *caro.*"

Nico dipped and kissed her on the forehead. "Thanks to you, my beautiful financial guru."

In the last year, they'd managed to infuse Gavretti Manufacturing with the cash it needed, sell off some of the Gavretti assets, and put the bulk of the estate back in the black. True to his word, Nico had put her to work right away in his accounting department—and he'd given her access to his entire fortune and all his business ventures. As a busy wife and mother, she often worked from home—and she loved what she did. Every day, she had her fingers in billions of euros worth of assets. And it felt damn good. She was proud of what she'd accomplished, and excited about what the future held.

"Faith called," she said as Nico bounced the baby. "They want us to come for dinner tomorrow."

"Then we shall go."

Tina smiled. It hadn't been an easy year for her brother and Nico, but they were learning to tolerate each other. Perhaps even to like each other again, though it was too soon to really know that for certain.

"I love you, Nico," she said, standing and hugging him and the baby both.

"You should," he teased. "Name another husband who would get up in the middle of the night to feed the baby while his wife slept."

She could think of a few—her brother most certainly, according to Faith—but she didn't say so.

"I think he's asleep," she murmured.

Nico looked down. "So he is."

They took him to his room and then lay him in the crib. Nico's fingers twined with hers as they stood there together and watched their son breathe.

"He is the most perfect thing I've ever done."

Tina slid her arms around him and kissed his jaw. "I'm sure I can think of one or two other things you do perfectly."

He turned until their bodies were melded breast to belly to hip, until she could feel the burgeoning evidence of his desire for her, until his lips slid along her throat and she gasped softly.

"Tell me what these things are," he whispered in her ear, "and I'll do them for you."

Tina shivered. "You might want to prepare yourself then," she said. "Because it's going to be a very long night."

He chuckled softly. "I'm counting on it, *amore mio*."

* * * * *

MODERN™

INTERNATIONAL AFFAIRS, SEDUCTION & PASSION GUARANTEED

My wish list for next month's titles...

In stores from 19th October 2012:

❏ A Night of No Return — Sarah Morgan

❏ Back in the Headlines — Sharon Kendrick

❏ Exquisite Revenge — Abby Green

❏ Surrendering All But Her Heart — Melanie Milburne

In stores from 2nd November 2012:

❏ A Tempestuous Temptation — Cathy Williams

❏ A Taste of the Untamed — Susan Stephens

❏ Beneath the Veil of Paradise — Kate Hewitt

❏ Innocent of His Claim — Janette Kenny

❏ The Price of Fame — Anne Oliver

Available at WHSmith, Tesco, Asda, Eason, Amazon and Apple

Just can't wait?

1012

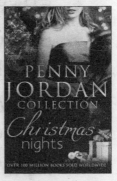